Color Me Dark

>─◆─◇─◆─◇─◆<

The Diary of Nellie Lee Love, The Great Migration North

BY PATRICIA C. MCKISSACK

SCHOLASTIC INC.
New York Toronto London Auckland Sydney
Mexico City New Delhi Hong Kong Buenos Aires

Bradford Corners, Tennessee
1919

Wednesday, January 1, 1919

Mama gave my sister and me diaries for Christmas, saying, "Every young lady should have a diary." I would have gladly sacrificed three toes and a finger to get some other "young lady" to take the little pink-and-white, ruffle-trimmed book off my hands. I put it in my chest of drawers because I had no plans to write in a book every day. I'd rather cipher numbers or, better still, I like working with wood alongside my Uncle, John Willis. He makes beautiful banisters, carved mantelpieces, doors, and of course all the coffins for our family funeral home business.

Now, my sister, Erma Jean, doesn't need to be convinced to write in her diary. She's been scribbling in hers since Christmas Day. She loves words the same way I love numbers. She plays with words all the time and says pretty things in poems and stories. She's made me promise to at least try writing in my diary. So I'm starting on the first day of the year.

"It's so much fun," says Erma Jean.

Can you imagine that?

Thursday, January 2, 1919

Erma Jean says I should write about what is important to me or interests me. Well, that's not so hard. My family is first. Then, after that, everything else interests me. I'm curious about all kinds of things from elephants to mosquitoes.

Erma Jean is my only sister. William is my only brother. William is away in the army — even though he just turned seventeen. Thank goodness the war is over and he is coming home soon. It's been so lonely without him and our uncle Pace who's soldiering in France. I'm so glad the war is over.

Later the Same Day

Most of the time I play with my sister. There are other children who live in Bradford Corners. They live miles away from town. Most of them are sharecroppers' children. Their families work the land for a share of the profit after the crop is sold. But most sharecroppers end up in debt no matter how hard they try. It takes everybody working to get the crops planted and harvested, so sharecropping children don't get to come into town for school, except in the winter when the crops are laid by, and in the summer, when not as many hands are needed.

Erma Jean is eleven and so am I. No, we're not twins, but Grandma Nessie — she's Daddy's Mama (Papa Till is his Daddy) — says we should have been, being born so close together and all. We're ten months apart. Erma Jean was born on February 28, 1908, and me on December 28, 1908. Can you imagine that? I came way too early and I only weighed three pounds. Daddy still talks about how he could hold me in the palm of one hand and none of me hung off the side. So that's how come two months out of each year my sister and I are the same age. Doesn't bother us none. But people who make comments about the way we look *really* bother me.

We're sisters but we don't look anything alike; I'm fair-skinned — like our Mama's people. Erma Jean is very dark like the Loves — those are our Daddy's folks. And William, our brother, is a mixture of the two parents — a warm, honey brown.

Some people are so color struck. They think being light-skinned is better than being dark! Mama says that's nonsense and I think so, too. I love it when Mama tells about her grandmother, Lizzie Palmer. She had been a slave. After the war, because she was so light-skinned many people thought she was white. But when people asked Lizzie Palmer if she was white, she'd always answer, "No, color me dark."

Daddy won't stand for color talk, either. He says a Colored family is like a beautiful bouquet of flowers — all different colors, sizes, and shapes. But each one just as beautiful in his or her own way. We only need to look at Daddy's side of the family to see that he's telling us the truth. The Love family is just like the bouquet Daddy described.

Wouldn't it be nice if everybody thought like Mama and Daddy? But they don't. Since Erma Jean won't speak up for herself, I've beat up more girls and a few boys, too, for calling my sister names — just because she's dark. But I can't fight grown-ups who say hurtful things. Like Grandma Nessie's sister, Aunt Minnie, on our father's side. We call her Aunt Meany. She never calls us by our names. She calls me the "Pretty One," and she calls Erma Jean the "Smart One." The last time she visited, Aunt Meany called to me, saying, "Come here, Pretty One." I pretended not to hear her. She called me again. I turned around and said, "Erma Jean, Aunt Minnie is calling YOU." Grandma Nessie got on me about being smart-mouthed. But later on, Mama told us, "Beauty is only skin deep."

Mama said a diary is a very private possession and that I should write things in it that I might not feel comfortable sharing with anyone else in the world. That would be hard for me to do, since I share just about everything with Erma Jean. We are blood, but she's also my best friend. I know the same red blood that runs in her veins runs in mine. But there is one thing I wish I could do. If I could, I would color myself dark. Then Erma Jean and I would look more like sisters on the outside.

Friday, January 3, 1919

Today is Mama's birthday. Erma Jean and I gave her an apron we made especially for her birthday. We made it during "quiet time." I know we are fortunate that our family has its own business and we don't have to share-crop, but sometimes I wish it wasn't a funeral home business! And more than that, I wish we didn't live upstairs over it! Then we wouldn't have "quiet times."

See, whenever there is a wake or a funeral going on downstairs, we have to be very still and quiet upstairs where we live. We can't make a sound. Daddy is very strict about that. If the floor squeaks just a little, he hurries upstairs to tell us to hush. There's a good reason why, though.

A few years back, Grandma Nessie was walking around cleaning upstairs while a funeral was going on. The family thought it was the ghost of their dearly departed. Folks started running over one another, knocking over chairs, trying to get out the door at the same time. It was a sight to behold.

So, from then on we've had to be still during services. In the summer it's not so bad. We play in the yard. But in the winter we have to do quiet things like write letters, paint, crochet, knit, or sew. For the past few weeks we have been secretly working on Mama's birthday apron. She put it on immediately. Mama's face is so pretty when it is glistening with happy tears.

Saturday, January 4, 1919

When it is storming, that's another time we have to be still. There is a terrible thunderstorm rumbling outside. Grandma Nessie has one rule everybody best follow if they want peace with her. "When God is doing His mighty work, we cease to do ours." I like it when there's a service going on at the same time it's storming. Then I don't have to be still twice. But there's no service here today.

Daddy just came in from helping Uncle John Willis

calm down Jupiter and Mars. They are the horses that pull the hearse. Both horses are jet-black, but Jupiter has a white mitten-shaped mark on his forehead. There's not a spot on Mars. Mars is nervous and gets storm-spooked easily. Daddy went out to make sure he didn't hurt himself.

Later

The storm passed, then it seemed to double back again. But we are all warm and snug inside this old house. I never knew my great-grandfather, who settled here in the Corners after the Civil War, but I thank him for building his house so big and strong.

I've wondered about Jasper Love plenty of times. His picture hangs at the bottom of the stairs next to a picture of his wife of many years, Lilly Tillman Love. Why for an instant did Jasper Love chose to settle in Bradford Corners when he could have moved east to Nashville or west to Memphis? Bradford Corners is south of Nowhere-in-the-World, Tennessee. There's one road in and one road out. The white folks live on one side of the road, and the Colored people live on the other. The white people call it Bradford. We Coloreds call it the Corners.

Yet how many times has Papa Till proudly told us how

his daddy started Love and Sons Funeral Home, back in 1879, with a few cents and a lot of faith, hope, and love.

Most Colored people here in the Corners look up to Daddy because he is a successful businessman. Mr. Leroy James, the Colored barber, is also well-respected. His house is four doors down from ours and his daughter, Josie James, is the only girl our age who lives within five miles of us. Daddy and Mr. James started the Colored Men's Improvement Association. Daddy's the president and Mr. James is the treasurer. And they are both trustees of the church. I guess in a lot of ways our fathers, along with a few others, are leaders in the Colored community.

Billy Collins is the only boy who lives close in. He's Miz Liza Collins's son. She cooks and keeps house for Mrs. and Mr. Lyle Stone, who is about the richest man in the state. Billy and his mama live on the place out back in a little bitty house. You'd never know Billy was Colored the way he talks about us so bad.

He says our house is crawling with haints and zombies just 'cause it's a funeral home. How would he know? Billy has never, ever set foot in our house. I'm not scared of dead bodies or coffins or even of the dark. Besides, Mama says evil can't stay around love. And there are enough Loves loving one another at Number 300 County Road for nothing unkind or wicked to stay around us long.

Sunday, January 5, 1919

It is early Sunday morning. The storm has passed over. Now it is just gray and cold. Daddy came into our room to put a lump of coal in our fireplace. It is his time to start the fire in the Baker heater at church so by the time services start the sanctuary will be nice and warm.

We don't have to get up for another few minutes. So, I am writing on my side of the bed and Erma Jean is writing on her side.

Jasper Love built a good house and a strong house. But it is a cold house! We sleep under two big quilts and my feet are still cold. Erma Jean complains all the time about how cold my feet are.

Later, After Church

As I bounced down the steps this morning, I spoke to Jasper Love's picture. "I was thinking about you last night," I told him. And as I walked through the rooms, I let my hands touch the dark framework in the receiving room, then I went into the small parlor, across to the large parlor, past the office, and the large back porch. In the kitchen, I try to imagine Lilly Tillman Love, Papa Till's Mama, baking bread. I see her standing beside Grandma

Nessie who was a much younger woman then. Her name was Honesta Pace, and she was Papa Till's new wife and Daddy's to-be-Mama.

I go up the back stairs, making a complete circle on the tour of our house. I pass by Grandma Nessie and Papa Till's bedroom where all six of their children were born — Freeman, my daddy, first; followed by John Willis; then Boston; Thannie — short for Beth Annie, the only girl; then Meese — short for Mitchell; and then Pace.

No, there are no haints and zombies in this house. It's a funeral home where we give the dead their last goodbye. But it is also a place where there's a lot of living going on, too.

Monday, January 6, 1919

Uncle Pace is Erma Jean's pick of the uncles. She calls him Uncle Brother, because she thinks of him more as her brother. Maybe it's because he suggested her name be Erma Jean after Mama's mother and grandmother. Uncle Boston is like a tree with roots that sink deep into Tennessee soil. He's slow-moving and slow-talking, but he's as steady and reliable as the rising sun. Uncle John Willis is good with his hands. Aunt Thannie went to live in New

York when we were little. She has her own school of music where she teaches piano and voice. Uncle Meese ran off when he was sixteen and he has lived in Chicago ever since. Neither one hardly ever comes home, so I don't know them too well. Daddy says Aunt Thannie and Uncle Meese are the strays in the family. He says that about William, too. William ran off before his seventeenth birthday and lived with Uncle Meese in Chicago, then put his age up so he could join the army like Uncle Pace.

I don't think I have a favorite relative. I love them all.

Later

Everybody admires Uncle Pace, and even though he is the youngest, his brothers look up to him — even Daddy, who is the oldest of the Love brothers. I remember them talking late into the night, making plans to expand the business and maybe even add a motor hearse and an insurance plan. But the war came. Now it is over and Uncle Pace is coming home!

Erma Jean and I share the bedroom near the back steps that lead to the kitchen. We often sit on the top steps and eavesdrop. We just listened to Mama and Daddy talking about the Ku Klux Klan. They scare me, because they don't like Colored people, and they don't like Jews or Catholics, either. Daddy says if the Klanners ever threw off their hoods and took a good look at one another, they wouldn't like themselves, either.

Sometimes before we go to bed, Mama and Daddy invite us into their bedroom, which is across from the room William and Uncle Pace shared. It's empty now. Daddy tells us a story then shoos us off to bed.

Papa Till does the opposite. He often asks me to read him the paper or a passage of Scripture. We just found out a few months ago that Papa Till can't read. He taught himself how to sign his name so he never has to make an X. He doesn't know we know, and Erma Jean and I have decided he never needs to know.

Can you imagine that? Even though Papa Till didn't get much schooling, he made it possible for all of his children to get a good education. Daddy finished school at Hampton Institute. That's where he met Mama.

Tuesday, January 7, 1919

Uncle Boston and his family came for dinner today. They own a farm out in the country about twenty miles away, and that's all they know how to talk about — work! The farm belonged to Aunt Celia's father and they inherited it when he died.

Every month or so Uncle Boston and Aunt Celia come to visit, or when Daddy needs help Uncle Boston comes in. Aunt Celia looks so tired all the time. But I guess I'd look tired, too, if I had three bad little boys underfoot and another one on the way. Uncle Boston goes on and on about how he wants four more boys and then maybe a girl. Poor Aunt Celia. I think she deserves a girl. A girl cousin would be wonderful to have.

Wednesday, January 8, 1919

We went back to school for the first time since the holidays. It's a little one-room, frame building, not as big as our house. On the way to the Colored School we pass Pough Elementary School. It's for whites only and it's made of brick. It has three teachers and a principal. Our Miss Brady teaches everybody, and she's the principal, too.

Today Miss Brady sent us home because rain was pouring through the roof so badly we couldn't sit at our desks. Daddy called a meeting of the Colored Men's Improvement Association. Erma Jean and I sat on the top step and listened to the meeting.

Miss Brady is the fifth teacher we have had in as many years. None of them stay very long. The first three teachers got married and had to stop teaching because it's the rule that married women can't teach. The fourth teacher missed her family and went back to Memphis. And now Miss Brady is threatening to leave unless the roof is repaired. So all the men promised to help fix the roof come Saturday noon.

Thursday, January 9, 1919

Uncle John Willis lives over the carriage house. His woodworking shop is behind it. People — both white and black — come from miles around to get him to make or repair their furniture. Uncle John Willis has the body of a man, but the mind of a little boy. But his heart is as big as a mountain. Some people say he is a bit addled. Mama says Uncle John Willis is slow and has been like that most of his life. People scare Uncle John Willis so much he stays to himself and works with his wood. "The wood don't bite," he says. So Daddy handles all of Uncle John Willis's affairs, because he can't manage on his own.

Uncle John Willis calls me Miss Mary Mack because I taught him how to hand-clap a new rhyme I learned.

Miss Mary Mack, Mack, Mack
All dressed in black, black, black
With silver buttons, buttons, buttons
Up and down her back, back, back.
She asked her mother, mother, mother,
For fifteen cents, cents, cents,
To see the elephant, elephant, elephant,
Jump the fence, fence, fence.
He jumped so high, high, high,
He touched the sky, sky, sky.
And he never came back, back, back
Till the Fourth of July-ly-ly!

It took me a while, but Uncle John Willis finally learned how to do the whole Miss Mary Mack hand-clap without one mistake.

It must be hard not being right in the head, like it's hard sometimes being the darker sister, the mother of three children under three, or the daughter of an undertaker.

Saturday, January 11, 1919

It has been a good day, not too cold. The men in the CMIA repaired the roof of our schoolhouse. It didn't take much, because it's just a small school — twelve regular students and maybe twenty-one when the weather's too bad to work in the fields and the sharecropping children come. But whether it's twelve or twenty we all have to fit into one room.

While Daddy was up on the ladder he straightened the school sign: COLORED SCHOOL. One of the things Daddy wants to do is get a new name for the school, but it has to be approved first. At least now, when we come on Monday, it will be dry inside.

Sunday, January 12, 1919

It was Quarterly Meeting Day at church today. At morning service, Reverend Greenlee preached from Genesis to Revelations and never seemed to take a breath. I got restless and Mama gave me one of her looks that says, "Be still!"

But I made up for it later. Erma Jean and I were on the program in the afternoon. I recited an eight-line poem by heart in front of the whole congregation. And I never missed a word. And I don't even like words the way Erma Jean does. She sang "Peace in the Valley," and she did a good job.

When we sat down, Grandma Nessie leaned over and

whispered, "Pride goeth before a fall, granddaughters." But when I saw the look on Daddy's face, I got tickled. Grandma Nessie should have been quoting Daddy that piece of Scripture.

My Daddy is a lot like his Mama. They both are as wide as they are tall. But Daddy is dark like Papa Till — as dark as tree bark wet with rain. Daddy is strong and when I hold his hand I feel safe. He is strictly business and when things are not done just so, he roars like a big lion — just like Grandma Nessie. Underneath Daddy is a gentle kitty cat. And so is Grandma Nessie.

Everybody in the family favors one of us — like Uncle Pace caters to Erma Jean and Papa Till is close to me. But Daddy never makes a difference between Erma Jean and me. He loves us equal. I love him best for that.

Monday, January 13, 1919

Some days Erma Jean is more sister than friend. Some days she's more friend than sister. I like it when we are both. Like today. We decided to get even with Billy Collins for teasing us about living in a haint house. I put some plain old ordinary dirt in a handkerchief. When Billy started his mouth to wagging, I tossed the dirt on him. "What was that?" he hollered.

I said in a spooky voice, "Cemetery dirt!"

"What will it do to me?"

Erma Jean grabbed her throat and gagged. "You'll find out," she croaked.

Billy called Erma Jean a black toad and called me a yella snake. For that we didn't even tell him we were just teasing. Let him stew in his meanness!

Miz Collins came by the house later this evening to tell Mama what we had done to Billy. Mama invited her inside, but she refused. Too scared, I supposed. Just stood there in the doorway looking wide-eyed over Mama's shoulder, like she was expecting a haint to float by any minute. Always a lady, Mama graciously assured her that she would speak to us. And she did.

But Mama gave us a chance to tell our story. I told how I had thrown the dirt. And Erma Jean showed how Billy's eyes bucked. She scolded us, then said that what we did was not ladylike.

Mama went downstairs to the kitchen. When she thought she was out of our hearing, we heard her burst into laughter.

>—◆>—O—<◆—<

Wednesday, January 15, 1919

There's a wake going on. "Quiet time" again — a good time to write.

We got a letter from Uncle Pace who's still soldiering in France. Daddy read the letter to us around the kitchen table this morning. It was dated October 9, 1918, before the November Armistice, but the letter just now got to us. Uncle Pace wrote that he couldn't talk about where his company was or what they were doing, but he could talk about the French people. Uncle Pace said the French are not like any whites he has ever known. They are kind, considerate, and very grateful to the Colored troops for helping them fight the war. He said a lot of the white American soldiers don't like the way the French admire us and praise us for being brave. So they told the French that Colored men have tails like monkeys.

Can you imagine somebody saying such a thing?

I wonder what Dr. W.E.B. DuBois of the National Association for the Advancement of Colored People would have to say about that. Dr. DuBois, who is the editor of the *Crisis* magazine that comes every month from the NAACP, wrote that Colored men should go fight for Democracy. Whatever the NAACP says to do, Uncle

Pace is likely to do. And whatever Uncle Pace does, William is bound to follow. So Uncle Pace enlisted in the army, first call. Last summer William got into a big argument with Daddy about going into the army. Daddy said he wasn't old enough and would not sign for him to enlist.

William ran off to Chicago. We woke up one morning and there was a note on the kitchen table. A few days later we heard from Uncle Meese who told us William was with him. But then in September, when he turned seventeen, he put his age up and joined the army. But the war ended in November, so he never saw action. Daddy was so mad at first, but all is forgiven now. William is in Washington, D.C., but we hope he will be home in a few months.

Uncle Pace didn't say when he'd be home, because when he wrote the letter the war wasn't even over. But he's got to come home soon. I know Grandma Nessie and Papa Till will be happy to see their youngest son. We all will.

Friday, January 17, 1919

In his letter the other day, Uncle Pace asked if Daddy was reading the *Crisis* to us the way he did. Uncle Pace was the first in our family to join the NAACP. Then he brought in Daddy and most of the men in the CMIA.

I will be happy to report that Daddy has been faithful. The first week in every month the *Crisis* comes. Daddy reads it from cover to cover and then again so as not to miss one comma or question mark. I love the articles, poems, stories, and all about what Colored people are doing, and what the NAACP is doing to make things better for our people. I'll be very, very happy when Uncle Pace comes home and he can share it with us again. Erma Jean is so excited she can't stop talking about it!

Sunday, January 19, 1919

Now that's a funny date — three nineteens in a row. There are going to be twelve three-nineteen dates this year — one every month. Erma Jean likes words. I like numbers. I like to play with numbers. So I've decided that on the three-nineteen days, I'll cipher with the 1, the 9, and the 3, and make up fun number games.

$$1 + 1 + 1 = 3$$
$$9 + 9 + 9 = 27$$
$$27 + 3 = 30$$
$$30 - 9 = 21$$
$$21 - 10 = 11$$

my age is

11.

Monday, January 20, 1919

Whenever possible, I slip out to the carriage house and watch Uncle John Willis work, but Mama doesn't like it. "Refined young ladies don't find themselves in wood-working shops," she says. I do, but I dare not say it out loud. Mama will not tolerate back talk. I'm always getting into trouble for having too much mouth. I'm trying, but that's another thing that's hard. It's hard not to question things. I wish my mouth had a key.

Friday, January 24, 1919

It's been a dreary and cold week — long, too. I'm glad it's over. One more stepping stone to spring. Billy Collins is now going around telling everybody that Erma Jean and I are witches. Said we put a hex on him. Most people know we are God-fearing people, so they're not likely to believe him. But he still makes me sick!

Saturday, January 25, 1919

Erma Jean and I got into a squabble early this morning. Erma Jean said I snored and kept her up all night. I said I don't snore. And besides, she slept like a wild woman and pulled the covers off me and I was cold all night. She imitated me snoring. I threw my pillow at her. She made snorting pig sounds. "I'm telling," I said, rushing down the steps to the kitchen. Mama and Daddy were at the table. "I'm telling, too!" she shouted.

I ran straight to Daddy and Erma Jean went to Mama. And the conversation went like this:

Erma Jean: Mama, Nellie Lee hit me with a pillow. What's the punishment?

Mama: For hitting your sister with a pillow, Nellie Lee Love, you will be sent to the attic where you will stay all day with just bread and water.

Oh, woe is me!

Me: Erma Jean said that I snored like a pig, Daddy. What are you going to do to her?

Daddy: Well, for insulting your sister, Erma Jean, I'm going to make you sleep in the root cellar where there are mice and spiders and roaches. . . .

Erma Jean: And then what?

We all laughed and clapped our hands.

Then, to save ourselves, we quickly said we were sorry and all was forgiven.

We've played this game since we were little girls. Mama and Daddy make up terrible punishments for some small wrongdoing. It helps us see how foolish many of our arguments are. We usually end up laughing so much, we forget what we were fussing about. Besides, we know Mama and Daddy would never carry out any of their threats — not in a million years, no matter what we did.

Monday, January 27, 1919

Erma Jean is asleep, but I can't sleep. So I am writing instead.

Earlier today, Erma Jean and I walked into town with Mama. We followed the train tracks down to the center of town. I love the spicy smell of cinnamon, nutmeg, and ginger that tickles my nose at the front door of Gunn's General Store. But that's all I like.

In the middle of the room there is a potbellied stove where three or four of Mr. Gunn's friends sit around, puffing on pipes and talking. In the summer they move to the front porch where they lean against the wall and carry on the same conversation they had last winter. They were all seated around the stove when we came in.

We know the routine. We stand just inside the door, quietly. Everybody knows we are there, but we can't move forward. It isn't that our feet are stuck to the floor. No. We dare not move! We have to wait until we are given permission to come in by one of the Gunns. After about four or five minutes (it seems much longer), Miz Gunn says to us, "Oh, hello, Olive. Girls. Come on in." It is as if she has just noticed us. The men around the stove never stop talking. We are invisible to them.

I asked Mama why we have to stand at the door like that. Her answer was, "It's just the way it is."

"But it makes no sense," I said. "Why do we go there?"

"There is nowhere else to shop."

"Maybe we should just go in one day without waiting for permission."

"Don't even think of it, Nellie Lee Love!" Mama said.

"Why?"

"No more questions. Do as I say!"

I still want to know why, but I don't ask anymore.

Tuesday, January 28, 1919

Erma Jean said Josie James told her that Sheriff Bell came to her father's barbershop and took out all the *Crisis* magazines. He warned Mr. James not to be caught selling them anymore. Said it was a magazine put out by anti-American people who put foolish ideas into the minds of Coloreds. Sheriff Bell told everybody in the barbershop that anybody belonging to the NAACP was asking for trouble and he wasn't going to be able to protect them.

Sheriff Bell did that? We'd always thought of him as a friend.

It sounded unbelievable to Erma Jean and me, so we asked Daddy.

After supper, Daddy explained that what we had heard was all true. In his own way, Sheriff Bell was trying to warn the Colored community that the Klan has added the NAACP to its hate list.

I remember Daddy reading the article in the *Crisis* to us that the Ku Klux Klan had reorganized a few years ago on Stone Mountain in Georgia. And they were getting stronger and stronger every day. Daddy warned Erma Jean and me to be very careful about what we said and what we did, because all the Klan needed was an excuse to harm somebody they didn't like.

Daddy told us that from now on we are never to mention that anybody in this family is a member of the NAACP or that we read *Crisis* magazine in the house.

"We'll still get the *Crisis*, won't we?" I asked.

Daddy didn't answer.

>─┤◆〉─O─〈◆├─<

Wednesday, January 29, 1919

It snowed today. It looks like sugar sprinkled on the ground, but it's just enough to make a snowball. On the way to school, the Braxton brothers chased Erma Jean and me. They threw snowballs at us. There are three Braxton brothers — George, Jeffrey, and Tommy. Tommy is the oldest and the meanest. We've been running from the Braxtons since we were little kids.

The County Road and the railroad tracks run side by side going east and west. On the south side of the County Road and tracks is the Colored section. On the north side is the white section. We never go on the other side of the tracks. Never. But sometimes the Braxtons catch us on the way to school and that always means trouble.

Today when Tommy Braxton was hurling snowballs at us, he was wearing a pillowcase with the eyes cut out — just like a Klansman. We knew it was him by his voice.

"Why don't you go tell his mother to leave us alone?" I said to Mama.

"It wouldn't help. In fact, it might do more harm."

"Why? Because they might be Klan?"

"No more questions."

>─┤◆├─○─┤◆├─<

Thursday, January 30, 1919

Got a wire from Uncle Pace. It simply said, *In New York. On my way home. Love, Pace.*

Saturday, February 1, 1919

Bud Simmons, the coal man, came today and left a load. I asked about his daughter Alice Mary. He says she and her sisters have been ailing. Alice Mary goes to school with us. She is quiet and shy and Billy Collins picks on her unmercifully.

After shoveling in the last of the coal, Mr. Simmons closed the coal shed and placed the lock on it. I offered to take the key, but he shook his head. "Miz Honesta" — that's what most folks call Grandma Nessie — "she would be all over me if I give somebody this key other than herself."

I ran to get Grandma Nessie. But she was busy, so Mama came. Bud Simmons would not be moved. He shook his head. "All due respect, Miz Olive. I know you lives here, but Miz Honesta told me never, ever to give this coal shed key to nobody but her." Mama turned on her heel and strutted away to get Grandma Nessie. She was still busy, so Papa Till came instead. Bud Simmons shook his head and backed away from him. "What did Honesta threaten to do to you that's got you scared enough to defy me?" Papa Till asked, half chuckling.

Bud Simmons didn't think it was funny. "I'm not crossing Miz Honesta," he said.

About that time, Grandma Nessie came swishing out of the door. She marched up to Bud Simmons, took the key, and marched away. "You'd think I was a terror," she mumbled. Papa Till looked at Bud Simmons and they both laughed. We all did.

Monday, February 3, 1919

Uncle Pace has not arrived yet. We keep a lookout for him. Papa Till has walked from the back to the front so many times, he's made a path. Grandma Nessie complains about his walking, but she's no better. If she pushes back the kitchen curtain one more time . . .

Tuesday, February 4, 1919

When a knock comes in the early morning hours, it usually means trouble. Sheriff Bell and four men from the Corners brought in Uncle Pace. "He's been bad hurt, Papa Till," the sheriff said. "Seems he got drunk and went to sleep on the railroad tracks and got hit by a train. That's all I can figure."

What? Uncle Pace doesn't drink! But we could smell the whiskey all the way at the top of the stairs.

Grandma Nessie went limp. Mama sent us upstairs before we could see anything. Daddy and Papa Till brought Uncle Pace's broken body up to his old bedroom. It had been readied for him with crisp and good-smelling sheets. Now those sheets are becoming his bandages — and maybe his winding cloth.

All night, Grandma Nessie and Mama have been taking turns sitting beside Uncle Pace. I begged to see him, but they won't let us into the room, yet.

Wednesday, February 5, 1919

Uncle Pace clung to life all day yesterday. Dr. Shipp finally arrived. He's the only Colored doctor to serve two counties and he was on the other side of the county delivering twins when Uncle Boston caught up with him. Daddy had gone into town to wire Uncle Meese, Aunt Thannie, and William to tell them to come.

Within a few hours, Dr. Shipp said he had done all he could do. He shook his head and left.

Thursday, February 6, 1919

It is dawn, first light.

Mama was exhausted. So she lay down for a quick nap. Grandma Nessie was with Uncle Pace. Erma Jean refused to sleep and sat in the hallway just outside his door. I sat with her.

Grandma Nessie called Erma Jean and me to come sit with Uncle Pace just a minute — just long enough while she fixed herself a cup of tea. We were glad to get to see him, especially Erma Jean.

When we saw Uncle Pace, my knees gave way. Erma Jean gasped and covered her face. When we had collected ourselves, we went over to the bed. "Oh, Uncle Pace. Don't leave us. Please," Erma Jean cried.

Suddenly, he moved. Then he reached out and took Erma Jean's hand. He was awake and trying to say something. I ran to get Mama and Daddy — anybody. It only took a few minutes, but by the time we got back Uncle Pace was dead. And Erma Jean wouldn't stop screaming. Then I realized she couldn't stop screaming!

Erma Jean and I have grown up around death. But today I saw Death for the first time face-to-face.

Later

Erma Jean hasn't spoken since Uncle Pace died. She wants to talk, but she can't — only *ga-ga-ga* sounds come out. Mama thought at first Erma Jean had screamed herself hoarse. But it's more than that. Erma Jean can't talk.

Saturday, February 8, 1919

My sister didn't utter a sound throughout the whole wake. Papa Till and Grandma Nessie are no better. She can't be still. He sits in his rocker reciting Psalms, searching for comfort. Daddy and Uncle Boston have had to handle all the arrangements. The wake will go on all day and all night.

People have been in and out of our house all day, bringing food that none of us is hungry for. Even some of the white ladies ventured across the road and tracks to bring a pan of biscuits, a piece of smoked meat, or a jar of preserves. Some had nothing to give, but they came to offer their respects. Relatives have come from all over the state. Josie's people are letting Papa Till's brother and wife stay with them. Even Aunt Meanie is here, staying with the pastor and his wife in the parsonage.

We're all sick with sorrow. Our eyes are puffy and swollen from crying. Even Uncle John Willis knows that Uncle Pace is gone forever. But Erma Jean just sits — no tears, no screaming. Just silence.

Later the Same Evening

Uncle Meese arrived on the 5:00 P.M. train in time for the wake. He was dressed in a suit and coat that looked like they cost enough to buy a motor hearse. Nobody ever says what Uncle Meese does, but whatever it is, he must be doing well — very well. Some of his childhood friends greeted him, "Good to see you," they said, "Sorry its for Pace. Too bad what happened." What happened? That's what we all want to know.

Aunt Thannie won't arrive until tomorrow. Uncle Boston and Celia are here with the boys. They've got me so busy I can't think straight. I caught the two-year-old eating ashes just a while ago.

Got word from William this morning. He is such a disappointment. He is refusing to come home. Says he can't stand to see Uncle Pace buried. What about us? We have to see it. I'm so mad at him! He should be here with Mama and Daddy, helping them to help Grandma Nessie and Papa Till get through all this. He should be here helping Erma Jean — and me.

Sunday, February 9, 1919

Instead of regular church services, we had Uncle Pace's funeral. Then we buried Uncle Pace in Zion Cemetery for Coloreds next to his grandparents, Jasper and Lilly Love. Aunt Thannie arrived just in time to walk with the family in the funeral procession. Daddy had trouble getting Jupiter and Mars settled down enough to pull the hearse. It took Uncle John Willis's gentle ways to finally put them at ease. When the drums signaled the beginning of the procession, Jupiter and Mars fell in line and pulled the hearse the quarter mile from the church to Zion.

It was so cold standing at the grave. Reverend Greenlee's words were kind and loving, but they didn't remove the hurt. Mama held Erma Jean's hand through the whole thing. And when my sister sobbed uncontrollably, Mama wiped her tears and hugged her up close. Grandma Nessie held my hand. I surprised myself at how still I stood, trying hard not to move. I felt like if I moved an inch, I'd start running and never look back at this place.

It was so cold. I don't think I'll ever be warm again.

Later

Erma Jean still hasn't said a word. Even the pretty scarf Aunt Thannie brought her from New York could not coax a smile out of her. Even the two nickles Uncle Meese gave her could not make her eyes shine again.

Tuesday, February 11, 1919

Daddy and Uncle Meese went to do business. Life has to go on.

I don't know when the idea came into my head that Uncle Pace had not been hit by a train. But that's what I'm thinking now. And I'm not the only one. Aunt Thannie doesn't think so, either.

The way he died makes no sense. First, he didn't drink. Second, he was too close to home to go to sleep on the railroad tracks. Something isn't right.

Sheriff Bell came by the house this afternoon. Mama knew it was going to be a grown-folks'-conversation, so she sent Erma Jean and me upstairs. We got to the top step and sat in the shadows where we could hear but not be seen. Mama, Aunt Thannie, Papa Till, and Grandma Nessie waited for an explanation.

Sheriff Bell said that Uncle Pace's death had been ruled an accident. Erma Jean squeezed my hand so tight I thought it would break. She couldn't talk, but she could cry. I wiped a tear from her eye and then she wiped one from mine. "I don't believe it, either," I whispered.

Aunt Thannie asked, "Do you really believe that, Lon Bell? You know Pace. Have you ever known him to take a drink of anything stronger than lemonade?"

She can speak to Sheriff Bell like no other person dares, because he practically grew up in this house. His Mama lived down in the Hollow where the whites and Coloreds are as mean as they are poor. They are known for being so ornery even the cottonmouth snakes go the other way when they hear them coming. Sheriff Bell's Mama worked hard to put herself up and out of poverty. But it was with our family's help that she was able to make it.

While Lon Bell's Mama went to school, he stayed with Grandma Nessie and played with young Thannie and Meese. And when his Mama got a job working for the only lawyer in town, Lon Bell still came to our house every day — and sometimes stayed over two and three nights. He grew up eating greens and cornbread at Grandma Nessie's table and following Papa Till around like a puppy.

Now he is sheriff and he was standing there telling Grandma Nessie and Papa Till that their son had died because a man who he knew didn't drink had gotten so drunk that he fell asleep on railroad tracks not half a mile from his house. And he had been so asleep he couldn't wake up and was hit by a train. Thannie wasn't having it!

Sheriff Bell: You're upset, Thannie.

Aunt Thannie: I have a right to be. My brother is dead and I want to know why and how it happened. One thing I know for sure, he didn't go to sleep on railroad tracks not a half mile from his house.

Sheriff Bell: Why can't you accept what happened? Let it go, Thannie, before you stir up a hornet's nest and get your whole family in trouble here.

Aunt Thannie: Is that a threat of some kind?

Papa Till: Sheriff Bell, I've known you since you weren't no bigger than a minnow. Tell me true. What happened to my boy?

Sheriff Bell: I don't know. There's some folks around here that's capable of doing harm. You've heard about the lynching over in Eastman? But I will swear on the grave you dug for my Mama that what I'm saying now is the truth. I honestly don't know what happened to Pace. But it wasn't the work of nobody around here for sure.

Papa Till was satisfied. But Aunt Thannie wasn't. Still she let it alone on account of Papa Till and Grandma Nessie who were upset enough.

After Sheriff Bell left, Aunt Thannie said, "When we women get the right to vote, we're going to vote incompetent people like that out of office."

Grandma Nessie shook her head. But Papa Till wasn't about to let that pass without comment. "Have you gone and got yourself mixed up in the hopeless cause of women's suffrage?" he said. "Don't you know, daughter, Colored women should be helping to get their husbands and sons the right to vote."

Aunt Thannie was not disrespectful, but she had her say. "Why not let Colored men and women work together to make sure *all* Americans have the right to vote in the North, in the South, East, and West."

Papa Till could not be convinced. Aunt Thannie went on. "Not only will women get the right to vote, I daresay a woman — perhaps a black woman — will be governor, mayor, representative, or even a senator in the United States Congress one day!"

Or president, I thought.

"Never!" said Papa Till.

I wanted to talk to Erma Jean about what Aunt Thannie had said, but she can't talk back to me. Even though we are still together all the time, I miss her so much.

Wednesday, February 12, 1919

When I took Uncle John Willis his lunch, he let me work with him in the shop. Usually he puts me to work sanding. But today, Uncle John Willis taught me how to use a tool that makes square pieces round. I went out back to choose a piece of hardwood to practice on when I caught Aunt Thannie smoking. Not a pipe or a cigar. Something smaller. She called it a cigarillo. Then she gave me a penny not to tell anybody. "I won't tell that you and Erma Jean sit at the top of the stairs and eavesdrop," she said, winking her eye, "if you don't tell you caught me smoking."

But I had to tell Erma Jean. I rolled up a piece of paper and imitated Aunt Thannie blowing smoke out of her mouth like a dragon. Erma Jean laughed. *Laughed!* I ran to tell Mama that Erma Jean was laughing. It was the best sound I had heard in a long time!

Thursday, February 13, 1919

Dr. Shipp thinks that Erma Jean will talk again. "Sometimes this happens. One day she stops talking. The next day she may talk again. Maybe. Maybe not. There's nothing I can give her to make her talk. She's got to want to."

Later

We're all worried about Papa Till and Grandma Nessie. Mama says they are grieving hard — each one in a different way. Papa Till sits and stares. Grandma Nessie can't sit still. Papa Till and Uncle Meese had a long talk today. Papa Till asked him to come home, help out Daddy. Uncle Meese offered to do anything Papa Till wanted or needed. "I'll buy you a motor hearse," he said. "I'll even take you to Chicago and you can retire, travel some. Just please don't ask me to come back South. I can't stay here. The Klan would lynch me in two days because I won't look at my feet while I'm talking to a white man or stand at the door waiting to be asked to come into a store I have enough money to buy!"

Papa Till was not happy with the answer. "If you stay in your place, you won't have no trouble here."

"That's it," said Uncle Meese. "I don't know my place. So it's best I stay in Chicago."

Friday, February 14, 1919

I can't stop dreaming about Uncle Pace. I just keep thinking I'm going to see Uncle Pace turn the corner of the house any minute. He'll come bouncing up the steps, smiling, telling some wonderful story about where he's been. Then I see people dressed in sheets running after him. I know them all even though their faces are hidden.

Saturday, February 15, 1919

There was a meeting of the Colored Men's Improvement Association at our house this evening. Aunt Thannie walked into the meeting without an invitation. She accused the men of being cowardly. Waving the February issue of the *Crisis,* she asked them, "How can you sit here trembling like rabbits while the Klan lynches people and the government does nothing? You're afraid even to say you are members of the NAACP, hiding behind the Colored Men's Improvement Association."

"We've got families, Thannie," said Mr. James, telling her to hold her tongue. "If we said we were members of the NAACP, we wouldn't accomplish what little bit we do. No need to bring trouble to our own front door."

Daddy asked Aunt Thannie to leave the room. Before going she asked, "Do you know how many black men, women, and children were lynched or murdered last year?"

When none of them could answer, she threw the *Crisis* at them and walked out.

Later

Erma Jean can't talk, but she's still curious. We wanted to know the answer to the question ourselves, so when the meeting was over, we tiptoed downstairs and got the February issue of the *Crisis*.

On the cover was a picture of a soldier in uniform. He looked so much like Uncle Pace, we almost thought it was him. Erma Jean touched his face with her fingers. So I knew she saw the resemblance, too.

Inside was an article: "Lynching Record for the Year 1918." And it listed month by month all sixty-seven lynchings that had been reported. No wonder Daddy had not shared this article with us. It is too horrible to imagine.

I don't believe Uncle Pace was hit by a train. I think he was murdered — and I think maybe Erma Jean might know something. When I ask her she closes her eyes and shakes her head violently. So I leave her be. But one day it will come out, Uncle Pace was killed.

Monday, February 17, 1919

Daddy decided to take Erma Jean to a doctor over at Meharry Hospital in Nashville. They left this morning and they'll be home tonight on the last train.

With Erma Jean and Daddy gone, I've just done a terrible thing. I looked through Erma Jean's diary hoping to find something that might tell me what she knows about Uncle Pace's death. She hasn't written a word since the day before his death. Nothing. I didn't look at another thing. Yet I feel so guilty.

When Erma Jean got home, I told her what I'd done. She looked surprised, then angry. She turned her back on me and that bruised my heart.

"I've just been missing you so much," I said. "I miss the way we talk about things and share our thoughts. I never know what you're thinking anymore." Tears filled my eyes. I was ashamed and sad.

Erma Jean wiped a tear from my cheek. And then I wiped a tear from hers. She had forgiven me. "I promise never to read your diary again," I said.

Suddenly, Erma Jean grabbed her diary and opened to a blank page. She fell across the bed and wrote:

I have an idea! I will write in my diary and you can read what I write.

"Do you really want me to do that?"
Erma Jean shook her head yes. Then she wrote:

I miss talking to you. I miss not being able to tell you what I'm thinking and feeling. Get a word in. This is the way we can talk. You speak to me. I'll write to you! I forgive you this time for reading my diary, but never, ever, ever, ever read my diary again, unless I say you can!

I was so happy that I'd been forgiven. I couldn't wait to ask her the question I wanted an answer to. "Did Uncle Pace tell you anything before he died?" I asked.

She scribbled across the page in big, bold letters.

And don't ever ask me that again, either!

Tuesday, February 18, 1919

The doctor said there was no reason why Erma Jean couldn't talk. Uncle Meese suggested that Daddy take Erma Jean to Chicago where doctors at Provident Hospital might look at her. Uncle Meese said he would even pay for the trip. He must really be rich.

Wednesday, February 19, 1919

It's a three-nineteen day again. Time to make up a new number puzzle using 3, 1, 9, 0.

91 is 19 backward
and
$91 + 9 = 100$
$91 + 9 = 100$
$91 + 9 = 100$
$3 \times 100 = 300$
and
300 is my address.
300 County Road
Bradford Corners, Tennessee

Thursday, February 20, 1919

We ran into the Braxton brothers again today. "Heard Erma Jean can't talk," one of them shouted. Then Tommy Braxton said the strangest thing. "Sorry to hear about your Uncle Pace." And for the first time that I can remember knowing the Braxtons, they let us pass without throwing a rock or chasing us.

Friday, February 21, 1919

Aunt Thannie left for New York this morning. At the train station she hugged Grandma Nessie and promised to write more often. She hugged Papa Till and teased him about being too set in his ways to travel. Although they disagreed on just about everything, she was still the only one who could bring a smile to his face since Uncle Pace's death.

Turning to Erma Jean, Aunt Thannie said, "I want you to meet some of my writer friends. You're every bit as talented as some of them." Erma Jean shook her head and smiled.

Then Aunt Thannie hugged me. "It's true you are the image of me when I was your age," she said. "And you've got my mouth, too. Just don't you ever be smart with me or I'll tan your hide." That made me smile. "Thanks for keeping my secret," she whispered.

"Thanks for keeping ours," I answered. "If Mama knew we were eavesdropping she'd switch our legs for sure."

"Board!" the conductor called.

And without another word, Aunt Thannie threw the fur wrap over her shoulder and dramatically held out her hand for the white conductor to help her onboard. It never crossed her mind that he wouldn't take her hand. Then she was gone.

>─┼─◆〉─◦─○─◦─〈◆─┼─◅

Monday, February 24, 1919

Uncle Meese is staying another week because he's waiting to travel back with Erma Jean and Daddy. She's going to be examined at the Provident Hospital, one of the best Colored hospitals in the country according to Uncle Meese. But Uncle Meese thinks that everything is better in Chicago. Of course he and Aunt Thannie disagree. She thinks that New York is the top of the world. I'd like to see both cities if I could.

They are going to leave a week from today.

In the meantime, Erma Jean and I are still talking and writing to each other. She wrote me tonight saying:

I wish you were coming with me to Chicago. I will write down everything so you can read about it when I come back!

Wednesday, February 26, 1919

The CMIA men met to discuss plans for naming the school. Mr. K.C. Morgan announced that he is leaving the Corners and moving to Cleveland, Ohio. "There's work there and better schooling for my children," he said. The Morgan brothers are younger than Erma Jean and me.

Mr. James put in, "I've heard Northern whites aren't any less prejudiced than these here in the South. They've had terrible race riots in Northern cities, too. And lynching! You remember the awful riot in East St. Louis, Illinois?"

"Brother James is right! I know my way around here," said one of the other men. "I don't know a soul up North. I reckon I'll take my chances here."

They all agreed that times are bad. Lynchings are on the rise. But they couldn't agree on whether it is better to stay in the South or go North.

"What do you think, Freeman?"

Erma Jean and I wondered what Daddy was thinking. He had been quiet during the discussion. "I'm taking my daughter up to Chicago next week, and I plan to give Chicago a good look. If what my brother Meese has been telling me is true, I might head North myself."

Erma Jean and I looked at each other in total shock. Daddy was thinking about moving to Chicago! What do you think about that? I asked Erma Jean. She grabbed her diary. She wrote in big, bold letters:

I DON'T KNOW. WHAT ABOUT YOU?

Thursday, February 27, 1919

I stayed awake thinking about Chicago. Do I want to go there? Do I want to live there? William had gone with Uncle Pace once to visit Uncle Meese. William never forgot it. Would it be that way for Daddy? When he sees it will he want to stay? And if he does, what will happen to Grandma Nessie and Papa Till and, most of all, to Uncle John Willis?

I'm not so sure about leaving the only house we have ever lived in. But I wouldn't mind getting away from Billy Collins or the Braxton brothers. Funny thing, though. Tommy Braxton said he was sorry about Uncle Pace. I wouldn't have expected that to come out of his mouth. But then there's Billy Collins. He's Colored, yet he hasn't said a word to us about being sorry. All he's done is tease Erma Jean about being unable to talk. "What's the matter, some other witch put a spell on you — throw some cemetery dirt on you?"

Erma Jean wrote me a note:

I'd live on the moon if it was away from Billy Collins.

>─┼─◆>─·─O─·─<◆─┼─<

Friday, February 28, 1919

It's Erma Jean's birthday. We are no longer the same age. She's twelve and I'm still eleven.

Mama made her a big cake and put strawberry preserves in the middle. Papa Till didn't break the tradition. When each one of his children turned twelve, he gave them a Bible. Now, Erma Jean, his oldest granddaughter, turned twelve, so he gave her one, too. He'd ordered it from a catalog from a store in Nashville months earlier to make sure the Bible arrived in time. Erma Jean was very, very happy. Her eyes were happier than we'd seen them since — since Uncle Pace. She wrote in her diary and showed it to me:

Today has been a good birthday. I am beginning to be happy again. A little.

Saturday, March 1, 1919

There's been a revival all week with Reverend J.M. Kopp, a prophet and faith healer. Grandma Nessie insisted that Daddy take Erma Jean up to be prayed over and anointed. Reverend Kopp cast out the demon of silence and told Erma Jean to speak. "Speak!" he shouted.

Erma Jean didn't say a word. Then the prophet accused Erma Jean of not having enough faith. Daddy was not pleased with that one bit.

Daddy brought us home. "Charlatan!" he said. Erma Jean and I didn't know what that word meant. Erma Jean looked it up in the dictionary. "Oowee," I said. "Daddy called Reverend Kopp a fake." *Charlatan.* That's a good word.

Sunday, March 2, 1919

Mama has been packing all day. I've been begging Erma Jean to write down everything she sees and hears!

Monday, March 3, 1919

Uncle Meese, Daddy, and Erma Jean left for Chicago. I can't remember a time when Erma Jean and I haven't shared the same bed. I am lonely. The feeling makes me scared, and I've never been scared in Jasper Love's house.

Tuesday, March 4, 1919

It was back to school — but without Erma Jean. Josie James is a good friend. We play tag and hand-clap together. But she's not my sister. Erma Jean will be home soon. But in the meantime it is back to arithmetic, spelling, and grammar. Practice. Practice. Practice. Every day the same thing.

> *I am,*
> *you are, and*
> *he, she, or it is.*

Mama was a schoolteacher for a summer when she was at Hampton, Virginia. Then she married Daddy. I just don't understand why there's a rule against married women teaching. Men teachers can be married.

Mama still teaches us a lot at home. She insists that Erma Jean and I use perfect English. Our verbs must agree with our subjects. And we can't slur our words or drop the g's off the "ings." We can't say huh and uh-uh. We can't shake our heads or shrug our shoulders. "Speak the king's English," Mama says when we try to get away with it sometimes. I want to ask her so bad, "Who is the king?"

Wednesday, March 5, 1919

Tonight the room felt small and stuffy, so I raised the window and sat on the windowseat. And now I am writing.

Winter is over, but there is a chill in the air. Can't help but think about Uncle Pace. Neither he nor any of the men hanged last year will see another lilac bloom or hear the robin's sweet song. Uncle Pace is gone. They are all gone.

Saturday, March 8, 1919

Daddy taught us an old saying: Red sky at night, sailor's delight, red sky at morning, sailors take warning. The sky was a blood red this morning.

Saturday, March 15, 1919

I haven't written since the tornado. On March 9, 1919, a tornado touched down and ripped through the Corners. Two people were killed — both Colored. Papa Till and Uncle Boston have been working overtime getting services ready.

Wind blew the roof off the carriage house, and Uncle John Willis had to hide under a table. Fruit trees were torn up by the roots. On the other side of the tracks, cows, chickens, goats, cats, dogs, and all kinds of animals were mixed in with wild things like foxes, rabbits, deer, and even a skunk.

Mars got out and broke his leg. Papa Till had to put

him down. Jupiter is so spooked he may not be any good as a carriage horse ever again. Papa Till says he'll finally have to break down and buy the motor hearse. But he's waiting until Daddy comes home to let him take care of it.

We are fortunate that our house was not damaged. Papa Till is proud of that. "The old house stood," he said. "It's built on a solid foundation of faith, hope, and love."

Of all times for Daddy to be gone. Mama took a letter to a man who is a train porter. He has a run to Chicago and happened to be in town. He promised to get in touch with Daddy through Uncle Meese. "Let them know we are fine," said Mama.

Where is William in all of this? I wondered. We haven't heard a thing from him. You'd think he would write, send word, come see us, anything. I am through with him! Really. Brother or not.

Monday, March 17, 1919

We are just now getting the March issue of the *Crisis*. Mr. James sneaked Mama a copy. Daddy stopped our subscription, so as not to call attention to us. Mr. James gets copies from the train porters who always have extras to sell. Sometimes they just give copies away to the people who can't spare a dime. It may not be a current issue, but it's all news to us. Mama read us a story and an article by W.E.B. DuBois about his trip to Africa.

Wednesday, March 19, 1919

It's a three-nineteen day.

> *If 191919 was money it would be:*
> *One hundred and ninety-one thousand*
> *Nine hundred and nineteen dollars.*
> *$191,919.00*
> *I would be as rich as Andrew Carnegie!*

Tuesday, March 25, 1919

Not much time to write. The weather's been good, so the whole community has been helping people to clean up and rebuild after the tornado. It was something to see white people and Colored people all working together, and talking to one another. How come we can't do that all the time?

Fortunately, the tornado didn't hit our school. But most of the children haven't been coming anyway. They're working in the fields, getting ready for planting.

Wednesday, March 26, 1919

Got a letter from Daddy. He's on his way home. He's leaving Erma Jean with a lady by the name of Mother Doris who is a good friend of Uncle Meese's. The doctors want to do more tests.

Mama doesn't seem one bit worried. I believe she probably knows more than she is telling. But Grandma Nessie and Papa Till are beside themselves. They can't imagine Daddy leaving Erma Jean behind in a big city with a stranger!

But Mama assured them that Daddy knows this lady and is comfortable with the arrangement. I am disappointed because I want to see my sister. I miss her so much it hurts. I don't want to cry, but I can't help it.

Tuesday, April 1, 1919

We haven't seen the Braxton brothers since the tornado. Their house was completely demolished. "Moved away," said Miz Gunn at the general store. "And they left a 50-cent bill here at the store."

So the Braxtons have moved away. I can't say I am all that sorry. But I can't forget that one moment when

Tommy Braxton spoke kindly about Uncle Pace. He went right back to being ornery, but it makes me wonder. Maybe being mean is a sickness he can't help. Sort of like Uncle John Willis can't help being slow.

Friday, April 4, 1919

Today is Good Friday, and school is out for spring break. Both the white and the Colored schools are in recess until June. Everybody is needed to help with the planting. Even people who aren't sharecroppers hire out to work during planting season. Then in June, when the crop is up, school starts again. Mama continues to teach us at home, though, so we don't get a break.

Sunday, April 13, 1919

Easter Sunday. Went to church and back home. The program was canceled because of rain. Grandma Nessie told me that if it rains on Easter Sunday, it will rain seven Sundays thereafter. I'm going to see if she's right.

➤ ⬩◆➤⬩○⬩◆➤⬩ ◄

Tuesday, April 15, 1919

Daddy's home! Daddy's home! Daddy's home!

Even though Erma Jean was not with him, it was so good to see Daddy.

The first thing I wanted to know was what the doctors at Provident Hospital had said about Erma Jean's voice. I could tell by the look on Daddy's face that the word had not been good. The doctors said Erma Jean might talk again and then she might not. That's what old Dr. Shipp had said, except the doctors at Provident gave her condition a name: hysteria. Daddy explained that Erma Jean got so upset—so shocked—when Uncle Pace died, she just stopped talking. It was too awful for her to speak about it.

That's what the doctors say, but I think it is something more. I wish Erma Jean would tell me what really happened. Why she won't talk about those last few minutes with Uncle Pace. One day she might tell me.

Later That Afternoon

Listening to Daddy talk about Chicago makes my toes tingle. He says some Colored people live in mansions on paved streets lined with trees. They have businesses of all kinds — places to eat and places to buy clothes. They own manufacturing companies. He told us there are automobiles going from one place to another on both sides of the street at the same time, and houses with running water, electric lights, and telephones — and none of these people are even rich. Can you imagine that?

Daddy went on and on about how Uncle Meese is doing very well. He has a fancy apartment and an automobile. He never really said exactly what Uncle Meese does. He's just in business — business doing what? I wonder.

Then Daddy told us that he had come back to get Mama and me, because he is planning to return to Chicago and open a funeral home.

Papa Till was shocked. "You talking about moving for good?"

"Why open a funeral home in Chicago when you have one right here?" Grandma Nessie added.

"It's not the same," said Daddy. "There are possibilities in Chicago that we can't even dream about here. It is a good thing for us to go."

Daddy was too excited to be turned around. He even has found the perfect place to open a business, he said. And he has put a down payment on an apartment. Mama must have known all along, for she is overjoyed.

I'm not sure what to think about the move. I have lived

in the house that Jasper Love built for his family all my life. The idea of me living somewhere else is like trying to see around a corner. I can only guess what's there. Daddy seems happy. Mama is happier, so I'm just going to trust that they know what's best.

Later That Same Night

Papa Till and Grandma Nessie are very unhappy about us moving. Papa Till said he always thought Daddy would take over the family business because Daddy "used to be" the level-headed son. He is surprised and disappointed that his oldest son has been swept off his feet by a pie-in-the-sky dream the big city promises. "The North is no better than the South," Papa Till argued. "At least you have family here."

"You have Boston," Daddy said, not changing his mind. "I'll have Meese. He's done very well away from here, and I intend to do the same. So with or without your blessing, Papa, I'm going to Chicago as soon as I can get my family packed and out of here."

"I can be ready in a day or two," Mama said, sounding as happy as a schoolgirl.

Sunday, April 20, 1919

A week has passed. We've been working nonstop, getting our clothes washed and ironed. Mama won't take a thing to Chicago that's not clean and fresh. It's as if she's trying to wash all the bad memories out with the dirt. It is good to get a rest.

It's Sunday and it rained this morning. A quiet rain. It was over by the time we got up and dressed for Sunday school. At church, Mama told me not to talk about our leaving — not just yet. But every day we are steadily getting things ready to go.

Tuesday, April 22, 1919

"Do they lynch people in Chicago?" I asked Daddy.

Mama looked in Daddy's eyes. "No," he said with confidence. "Things are different than they are here. We're going to a far better place than this little corner of darkness," he said.

Wednesday, April 23, 1919

We heard from William today. He's been given an early discharge from the army and he's working in Baltimore.

He plans to stay there for the time being. He says he is sorry for not coming home for the funeral, but he just couldn't face the death of Uncle Pace. Then William wrote something that shocked us all.

> *Pace was not run over by a train. I believe he*
> *was murdered. Terrible things are happening to*
> *returning soldiers all over. Some have been*
> *found beaten and hanged while still in their*
> *military uniforms. You all be very careful.*
> *Times are bad! Very bad.*
> *Love,*
> *William*

He wasn't even here, yet he feels the same as we do. Uncle Pace did not die the way Sheriff Bell tried to convince us he had. We may never know what really happened. I can't help but think Erma Jean may know something.

At least we have an address for William. In spite of myself, I was glad to hear from him. Mama answered his letter, telling him about our move to Chicago. I didn't add a word because I am still mad at him — but not really all that mad anymore.

Thursday, April 24, 1919

Grandma Nessie announced that she was giving Mama her stem crystal — the set of twelve glasses that had belonged to Grandma Lilly and Grandpa Jasper Love. Mama was overwhelmed and didn't know what to say. "I want you to have these to dress up your dining table while you're entertaining all those important people you're bound to meet in Chicago city."

Lovingly, Mama and I carefully packed each crystal glass and Mama says she's going to hand-carry them with her.

Saturday, April 26, 1919

I went strawberry picking with Grandma Nessie. And I've been itching all night because the mosquitoes ate me alive! "Do strawberries grow in Chicago?" I asked.

"I 'spect they do," Mama answered.

"But they'll never be as sweet as the ones here," Grandma Nessie added.

I wonder.

><+>·O·<+><

Sunday, April 27, 1919

Papa Till invited Reverend Greenlee to have dinner after church. It didn't take long for the reason to be known. As soon as grace was said, Reverend Greenlee started in on how it was sinful for Daddy to stray away from his parents. He said Chicago was like Sodom and Gomorrah in the Bible. When the Reverend was gone, Daddy's mind was still made up. "We're going to Chicago."

Grandpa Till was still ready to argue. But Grandma Nessie stepped in. She told Papa Till that he couldn't hold on to Daddy like a child. "Freeman is a grown man, the head of his own household. You got to let him stand tall and be a man. God knows this world won't let a Colored man rise too high lest it knock him down. So let him be a man in his own house."

Papa Till left the room in a huff. He didn't come back until everybody was asleep. Thunder woke me up. It is raining again on Sunday. I heard Papa Till come in. I sat on the top step and listened to him pour a glass of something to drink — milk probably. It isn't nearly as much fun eavesdropping without Erma Jean. But in the quiet of the kitchen I heard my grandfather cry.

Thursday, May 1, 1919

Today was May Day in the Corners. Every year in the spring, the whole Colored community celebrates the first day of May. Grandma Nessie says it is because we've made it through winter and we are thankful and should celebrate. Mama and all the other ladies bake pies and cakes. There are horseshoe games, footraces, and ring tosses. Ladies show off the quilts they made all winter and some of their fine stitching, knitting, and crocheting.

A few white people come to buy a quilt or a basket, but they never stay long or participate in anything we do. They're welcome, even though we would never be welcome at any parties they have.

The only white person who comes to May Day and stays the whole time is Sheriff Bell. He's been coming since he was a little boy. "Heard you all are leaving, going up North," Sheriff Bell said to Daddy. "I've thought about leaving plenty of times," Sheriff Bell went on. "But my roots are here, planted deep, too deep to dig up now."

Daddy nodded. "It's not going to be hard for me at all," he said, taking my hand to join the three-legged race.

Long about evening time we always have a May Day program, and in the end the children wrap the Maypole and crown the Little Miss May Day. That's whoever sells the most penny tickets. This year Doris Mason was Little Miss May Day. She cheated! I know she did.

I worked so hard for Josie James to win. We were always friends, but since Erma Jean has been gone, Josie and I have become closer. I sold penny tickets everywhere and we raised 55 whole cents. Lela Lewis asked me how much we had raised, and I told her. Lela said she had raised 6 cents and Doris had raised 54 cents. When it was time to report the money, Lela turned in 4 cents. And Doris turned in 56 cents. You don't have to be a genius to figure out what happened. Doris only had 54 cents. Lela gave her two of her pennies to make her have 56 cents and enough to beat Josie.

"Who wants a dark-skinned Little Miss May Day?" I overheard Lela tell one of the other girls. Before I could talk myself out of it, I had flown into Lela, arms flying like a windmill. Reverend Greenlee snatched me off her and spanked my hands in front of everybody. Mama was scandalized when the preacher marched me up our front steps and into the house. He told her that I'd disgraced myself by fighting in the churchyard, of all places. This time Mama looked really disappointed in me.

"Daughter," she said, "you can't take on the world."

"I don't understand," I said. "Why do light-skinned

Colored people think they are better than dark-skinned Colored people? Aren't we all Colored? I think it's stupid and wrong."

"Even if that's true, two wrongs don't make a right," Mama said as she switched my legs and sent me to my room.

Saturday, May 3, 1919

Our days have been filled with making strawberry preserves and putting in Grandma Nessie's kitchen garden. Then we help Mama pack. I will miss Grandma Nessie's fried green tomatoes and fresh biscuits on Saturday morning.

Sunday, May 4, 1919

There was a basket social at the church but it got rained out. We had dinner on the Jameses' back porch. Josie and I got a good laugh. "Thanks," she said, "for taking up for me about the Little Miss May Day money."

"People like Doris Mason make me sick," I said.

"And don't leave out that dreadful Billy Collins," Josie added.

I will honestly miss Josie, but I won't miss Billy Collins. Poor Josie is going to have to put up with him all by herself. At least she doesn't have the Braxton brothers to bother her anymore.

Friday, May 9, 1919

We heard from Uncle Meese today. He is so happy we are coming to Chicago. He said Erma Jean is doing fine, but she misses us very much. She is especially enjoying her stay with Mother Doris. I found out Mother Doris lives in the same building where we will be living. We are to wire Uncle Meese when our train will arrive. He said he will meet us at the Chicago train station.

Saturday, May 10, 1919

There was a funeral today. But at least I could play outside instead of having to sit quietly upstairs. Later, I spent time with Uncle John Willis. He covers his ears when I try to talk to him about us leaving. He won't listen, the same way Erma Jean won't talk. Nobody seems to own up to what's bothering them.

Sunday, May 11, 1919

Papa Till has finally come to peace with our going. He gave Daddy his blessing and a sum of money.

Papa Till: You helped to earn it, so take this and get that new start you're dreaming of.

Daddy: This was the money you were saving to buy a motor hearse.

Papa Till: I've held back enough to replace Mars. With John Willis's love and gentle care, I think Jupiter will last a little longer.

Daddy: I was thinking of naming my business Love Funeral Home of Chicago. But I think I like "Love and Sons Funeral Home, North."

Papa Till: I like the sound of that very much. But one thing more. Promise me that if Chicago is not good for you or your family, don't let your pride stop you from coming back home. This is home and we are always here ready to welcome you back any time you need to come.

It feels good falling to sleep with the sound of rain hitting against the windowpanes and hope in my heart.

>-+->-O-<+-+-<

Sunday, May 18, 1919

It was as hot as July today. Will it rain like Grandma Nessie says it's supposed to?

Uncle Boston, Aunt Celia, and the boys came over to say good-bye. They are going to give up the farm and move in with Grandma Nessie and Papa Till. That way it won't be so lonely for them and maybe Celia will have some help.

Later

It is pouring down cats and dogs. Grandma Nessie has been right so far. It rained on Easter Sunday and it has rained for five Sundays thereafter. Two more to go, but I'll be gone. I'll have to remember to write home for the answer. Funny saying I should write home. Bradford Corners is not going to be home for me much longer. Chicago will be home.

Monday, May 19, 1919

We are leaving on a three-nineteen day. Three nineteens add up to 57. And that's the number of the coach we are on. Saying good-bye to everybody was the hardest thing I've ever had to do.

Uncle John Willis was a puddle of tears when he gave me a little wooden angel that he had carved out of cedar. "Hang this in your closet and the moths and mildew won't get your good clothes." We played Miss Mary Mack one last time and then I hugged him and Jupiter and ran away as fast as I could.

Grandma Nessie gave Mama a big hug and smiled as best she could. "This house will be empty without my girls," she said.

"You can come see us in Chicago anytime," said Mama.

"We'll see." That was Papa Till's way of politely saying no. Papa Till had never been out of Middle Tennessee. Chances are he won't come as far as Chicago.

5:00 P.M.

We left the Corners on a local at 3:00 P.M. We got to Nashville at 4:30 P.M., where we have a three-hour layover. The Colored waiting room is crowded and stuffy. I wonder, does the white waiting room smell of fried chicken and deviled eggs mixed with body odor? Would my head feel any better over there? I've tried not to be fretful, but it is hot and uncomfortable. Small children are crying. Mama reminds me that I am not a baby. It is the longest three hours of my life.

8:30 P.M.

We just left Nashville and we are on our way to Evansville, Indiana. It is hard to write on a rocking train. But it is even harder to sleep. I've never been this far from home. Just when I feel like I can't go on, I remind myself that Erma Jean had made it and so will I.

We were fortunate that we all got seats together. Daddy let me sit by the window. He's sitting on the aisle. Mama is on the aisle seat across from him. There is a woman sitting next to Mama with a small baby. The baby is sick and cries all the time. Mama is helping the lady.

Mama unwrapped some fruit and a few slices of pound cake. Papa asked a porter what time it was. He told him it was 10:45. I like the way the porters say 10:45 rather than a quarter till eleven.

One of the porters asked us where we were from and if we were going to St. Louis or Chicago. Daddy told him Chicago. Then the friendly porter looked at me. "Well, hello, little princess," he said. "You look like you might be from Hawaii."

"No, I'm just a Colored girl," I said.

"Well, you ought not to tell anybody," he said, "'cause you could pass if you wanted to."

I folded my arms. "I don't want to pass," I said. "You can just color me dark," I added.

Mama gave me the look that says I am being smart-mouthed. The porter smiled and moved on.

1:30 A.M., Tuesday, May 20, 1919

I woke up when we reached Evansville, Indiana. The train we were on will go into St. Louis. We changed trains for the one that will take us into Chicago. It leaves at 3:30 in the morning.

The train going to Chicago is crowded. Daddy and I are seated two rows behind Mama. There are soldiers getting on board. Two of them remind me of Uncle Pace and William. I shake the thought out of my head. We are leaving all that behind us. Chicago is a new place, a place where bad things don't happen just because of your color.

>—I—◇—O—◇—I—<

6:00 A.M.

The train was late leaving Evansville. I leaned on Daddy's shoulder and went to sleep. It is now morning. I am writing as the sun rises on my right, so we are moving north — north to Chicago.

I am so hungry. Daddy got off in Evansville and bought some sandwiches. But that was hours ago.

We are sitting across from a gentleman who looks so distinguished. I imagine he could be one of the famous Colored people — like Dr. W.E.B. DuBois or maybe even James Weldon Johnson. He isn't one of them, but it's fun to imagine. What would I say to Dr. DuBois? "Sir, think the *Crisis* is the best magazine ever, and I hope you do more *Brownie* editions for us children. It's my favorite of all the *Crisis* issues."

The man across from us is sitting poker straight, with his arms folded across his chest, as if to protect himself from some coming blow. Another man just lit a pipe. It makes me cough and sneeze. Daddy asks the smoker to please step out on the landing to smoke. "Have you no sensibilities for the ladies and children in the car?" Daddy says. The smoker grumbles something and excuses himself.

The man next to us turns to Daddy. "Bravo," he says.

"What a pleasure to meet a gentleman in this cattle car. Traveling conditions are insufferable! I am Gregory Hill," he says, extending his hand. Daddy shakes his hand and pardons the fact that he is still seated. "Freeman Love, and this is my daughter, Nellie Lee."

"Ah," says the man, his face full of interest. "The Loves of Nashville?"

"My father always says we are related in some way. If not by blood, then by plantation for sure," Daddy says, smiling.

The light goes out in Mr. Hill's eyes. But he remains cordial. "I'm in banking," he says. Daddy replies that he owns a funeral home. Mr. Hill seems interested again.

Mr. Hill goes on to say he is returning from a visit to Kentucky where his aging mother had just passed. He has lived in Chicago for thirty years and says he has no intention of moving South again. Daddy is interested in what Mr. Hill has to say about Chicago. I am, too. I stop writing to listen.

Mr. Hill gave us an unexpected view of Chicago. He said the city was nice before the war and race relations were good. But now the city was being overrun by poor, ignorant Negroes, and race relations had turned sour. "Look at them," Mr. Hill said, pointing to the people around us. "They bring disgrace to the whole race by their common ways, superstitions, and loose morals. They have nothing and want nothing but a big time. Those of us who have worked hard to build a little something for ourselves are not being lumped into one bag with these . . . these people."

With my eyes closed Mr. Hill was saying many of the things I have heard whites say about us. He gave Daddy his number and told him to visit his bank. Daddy said he would, but I don't care if we ever see Mr. Hill again.

9:30 A.M.

The conductor announced that we were entering Chicago. But it took us forty-five minutes to actually get into the station. I looked out the window the whole time, my face pressed against the glass. Chicago is an amazing place — not like any place in the whole wide world. And it's my — our — new home.

Chicago, Illinois

Later On That Day

We are in Chicago!

I've never seen so many people — all kinds of people from different countries coming and going in the train station. Many of them were dressed in clothing I have never seen anybody wear before. Some were greeting passengers and talking in different languages. Although I don't know what some of the people were saying, I understood their expressions of joy and happiness. They were glad to be in Chicago, too.

And Colored people were at the station, too. Some families were large and some were small. Some were well dressed and some weren't. But all of them had the same wide-eyed expression that was on my face. They were happy and scared at the same time. I couldn't wait to see Erma Jean! It has been so long — too long.

The train station was like a city all by itself — a city with a roof over it. But outside the station there was a city that seemed to stretch on and on forever. Buildings and buildings behind those. Streets that go all the way to the ends of the earth. And there were motorcars whizzing past, going over twenty-five miles per hour. Can you imagine that? Mama kept telling me to shut my mouth, but when I looked, hers was as wide open as mine.

Uncle Meese didn't meet us, but he sent a man for us in a motorcar. Daddy introduced him as Mr. Link, one of Uncle Meese's employees. Mr. Link is a tall, dark-skinned man, with a nose that looks like somebody stuck a ball on the end of it. His eyes are bright and his smile is slow to come but sunny. He greeted me with a tip of his hat and a wink. "I know somebody who's been missing you," he said.

I knew who Mr. Link was talking about. "Are we going to see Erma Jean now?" I asked.

"Be patient," Mama said. "We'll get there when we get there."

Mr. Link drove us down paved streets where beautiful houses stood stately and grand on each side. I had been in a motorcar before but not on a paved street. There is only one paved street in the Corners, and it is only two blocks long. All along the way, Daddy pointed out places he remembered from his short visit, and Mr. Link filled in the rest.

At last we arrived at the apartment building at 2606 State Street. It is a three-story, six-family building. "Where is Erma Jean?" I begged.

Suddenly, she came rushing out the door and hurled herself at Mama and me. She had only been away about eleven weeks, but she seemed taller, older to me. She clapped her hands and tried to make sounds, but no words came out. That part hasn't changed. Daddy told me that the Provident Hospital doctors said that she is going to have to make up her own mind to talk. She'll talk when she's ready. I still think it has something to do with the way Uncle Pace died.

But Erma Jean didn't have to say anything. I understood she was happy to see us. And she could see I was overjoyed. "I have so much to tell you," I said, hugging her tightly. She shook her head and laughed!

Mother Doris was the first person we met on State Street. Her warmth and loving spirit is very comforting. She welcomed us to a meal she'd prepared of ham, potato salad, and homemade rolls. "Go get settled in your place, then come down and have a bite to eat. I knew you would be hungry," she said.

I liked Mother Doris right away. She has a calm, kind way that makes everybody around her feel comfortable. No wonder Daddy felt good about leaving Erma Jean with her. Can you imagine? Erma Jean has been staying with this wonderful lady while I was putting up with Billy Collins. Doesn't seem fair.

Daddy brought us upstairs to our furnished apartment. It is nothing at all like the house that Jasper Love built. Oh, it is neat and clean, but so very tiny. It only has two rooms in it — a bedroom and a kitchen-living room-dining room all in one. Erma Jean and I sleep on cots that fold up during the day. They're a lot different from the big four-poster bed we have shared all our lives.

The front window is a bay window with lovely lace curtains. It overlooks the street where a steady stream of people — all strangers — pass by in a hurry going to heaven knows where, and noisy motorcars chuck-a-long at breakneck speed.

Daddy showed us the toilet that we will share with the other family who lives on the second floor. Now the house that Jasper Love built doesn't have an indoor toilet, so it's going to be nicer than an outhouse. I pulled the flushing cord just to hear the water swish! Erma Jean giggled. We have electric lights here — same as we did in the Corners. There is no yard to play in though, no large trees to climb and swing on. But Daddy says there's a park right around the corner and Lake Michigan is a short streetcar ride away.

If Mama wasn't satisfied with anything, we couldn't tell. "With a few of our personal things here and there, I think we can make this into a home," she said, smiling.

Daddy seemed relieved. "We won't be here too long," he said. "As soon as I get established, we'll move to another . . . better apartment. Maybe even buy a house."

He picked up Mama and turned her around and around. Erma Jean and I joined in the excitement. We were in Chicago and even though we have less in some ways, we seem to have more in other ways. After Daddy gave each one of us a big hug, we hurried downstairs to eat some of Mother Doris's ham and potato salad. I was starved.

Wednesday, May 21, 1919

First thing Mama made us write Grandma Nessie and Papa Till and let them know we are fine. I asked Grandma Nessie to let me know if it rained on the sixth and seventh Sunday after Easter.

Later

I met Rosie Hamilton today. She lives on the first floor across from Mother Doris. And like me, she's eleven years old. Rosie is funny and talkative and I like her. She knows a lot about the neighborhood.

"I'm Erma Jean's sister. I'm Nellie Lee," I said.

"I'm Rosie," she told me. "And I can sure tell you're

from the country. Only country people have two names. You're in the city now — you need to drop one of those names."

About that time, Mrs. Hamilton called from the window, "Rose Marie, it is time for you to come in for supper."

Rosie sighed! "Oh, Mother. Please call me Rosie."

"Mother?" shouted Mrs. Hamilton. "When did you stop calling me Mama?"

Erma Jean and I laughed until we were breathless. Then I asked, "Do you want me to call you Erma?"

To my surprise, Erma Jean shook her head yes. Can you imagine? "Well, then maybe I ought to be Nell. We don't want to look like we fell off a turnip truck."

Later

Erma showed me her diary so that I would know what had been going on while we were apart. On May 12, 1919, she entered a poem:

> *Chicago is not like home.*
> *Is it better or is it worse?*
> *I'm not sure, yet.*

It might be our best hope.
But Chicago could be a curse.
Who knows.
Chicago is home
but not the home in my heart.

"I feel that way about Chicago, too," I said. "I *want* to like it."

Erma shook her head again harder.

Thursday, May 22, 1919

We wash up every morning in a face bowl in the toilet. We will still have to take baths in a tin tub in the kitchen on Saturday nights. Mama has promised to switch my legs if I play with the pull cord in the toilet again. I love the sound of it swooshing the water down into the pipes. SWOOSH!

Later

Back home in the Corners there was a big tree out back that had birds, squirrels, and possums living in it all together. William found a snake up there one time. This building reminds me of that tree. Rosie knows everything about everybody who lives here. She told us about them today.

Virginia and Thomas Kebbs live on the third floor at #3-North. He's an intern over at the Colored hospital, Provident Hospital. That's where Erma is being treated for her condition.

Mr. and Mrs. Williams, from Lexington, Kentucky, live at #3-South, with their son, Eugene. He and his father are porters for a big insurance company. Mr. Williams works at night; Eugene goes out every morning at seven o'clock. Rosie says Eugene is working to save up enough to get his own apartment.

John and Bessie Martin moved in a week before we did into #2-North. They came from Jackson, Mississippi. Rosie doesn't know a lot about them. We live at #2-South.

Mother Doris lives on the first floor at #1-South. Her husband died of the flu this past winter, so she lives alone with her cats, One Cat and Two Cat. Erma wrote me that Mother Doris's cats are spoiled but lovable. We never had pets at home, except maybe Mars and Jupiter. Daddy said dogs and cats don't fit in well at a funeral home. Even Jupiter and Mars were workhorses and not to be treated as pets. But Erma and I would slip out and hug them anyway. Rosie said she had lots of pets back in Arkansas. She even had a pet pig.

I can't imagine such a thing.

Rosie and her Mama live in #1-North, right across from Mother Doris. I found out from Mother Doris that they've only been here a few months, too. You would think Rosie had been born in Chicago the way she gets around and knows so much.

Mama thinks Rosie's mama allows her too much freedom. "I just don't think it is appropriate for an eleven-year-old girl to come and go at will," Mama told us. "I'll not have you girls running loose like March hares. No indeed!"

Friday, May 23, 1919

Uncle Meese came by the apartment today. Mr. Link helped bring in presents Uncle Meese brought for everyone — Mama, Erma Jean, and me. He even gave Daddy a new watch chain. It was just like Christmas — no, better than any Christmas. Daddy said he was spoiling us, but Uncle Meese wouldn't hear of it. He has to be doing something very important, because he dresses well and has people working for him like Mr. Link.

Uncle Meese was full of apologies for not meeting us

at the train station. "I had a meeting with a very important client, but I trust that Mr. Link saw that you were taken care of," he said.

"What do you do for a living?" I blurted out before thinking. Mama gasped. Uncle Meese started to answer, but Daddy told me that I asked entirely too many questions, then he sent Erma and me out to play. Erma was mad at me but she only told me with her eyes.

Now I'm really curious. What *does* Uncle Meese do that Daddy doesn't want us to know about?

Sunday, May 25, 1919

Today Mama and Daddy dressed us in our Sunday best and we went looking for a city church. Back home we were A.M.E. Mama didn't care where or what denomination it was. She just wanted us "churched," as she called it.

A few blocks away on 28th Street we passed a sign that said: THE OPEN MIND CHURCH AND YOUTH CENTER. REVEREND PRINCE MCDONALD. An arrow pointed down to the basement.

Mama liked the sound of the music and led us in. Daddy followed, but he wasn't all that happy about it.

There were about fourteen people worshiping in the happiest way. I heard Erma suck in her breath. I followed her gaze and stopped breathing for a second or two myself. Hanging on the wall behind the preacher was a Colored Jesus as dark as any Colored person I have ever seen. I couldn't take my eyes off Erma who couldn't take her eyes off the picture.

Reverend Prince McDonald is a young man in his twenties, but he has a way that makes him seem older than his years. And his sermon was like nothing I had ever heard.

"We are told to love one another, but if we don't first love ourselves, how can we care about others with a richness of spirit?" Mama sat on the edge of her seat the whole time he was talking.

When services were over, he shook Mama and Daddy's hands and invited them back again next Sunday. When he met Erma he gently lifted her face. "I noticed you looking at the picture of our Lord," he said. "It is a very special picture, isn't it?"

Erma nodded her head. "She can't talk," I said. "Got hysteria."

Erma flashed me a dirty look. I shut up quickly.

"Did you paint it?" Mama asked.

"One of my students did," he said. Then he asked if Mama and Daddy would allow us to come to his classes next Saturday. He holds a youth lecture series from one o'clock until three. Then regular church services on Sunday.

Mama was impressed with Reverend McDonald. So it didn't take too much to convince Daddy that we could go to the lectures on Saturday.

Erma wrote me later tonight:

I like Reverend McDonald. I feel he is a kind and good man. I also love the picture of the Colored Jesus. I'm looking forward to next Saturday when we can go there again.

Me, too! He doesn't seem to be a charlatan.

Tuesday, May 27, 1919

Erma and I don't have to eavesdrop anymore. We can lie on our cots at night and hear everything that's being said in the apartment across the hall, upstairs, downstairs, and outside, too. This is a very noisy place.

Wednesday, May 28, 1919

Erma and I have been doing some investigating into Uncle Meese. We asked Rosie if she knew anything.

"No," she said, "but Mother Doris would. After all, he stayed with Mother Doris when he first came to Chicago." See! We didn't know that.

We found a reason to visit Mother Doris's apartment. One Cat jumped in my lap and insisted that I give him a back rub. We tried to pick for information about Uncle Meese, but Mother Doris wasn't talking. So we stopped trying and enjoyed her cinnamon rolls.

Saturday, May 31, 1919

We know our way to the market store and back. And we know how to get to the park. But Mama walked us to Reverend McDonald's Open Mind Church and Youth Center. She stayed a bit to hear what his lecture was about.

There must have been five or six children and two or more adults in the small basement room. "This is our third lecture in the series," he said. "But already we have two new children and their mother." Everybody applauded, which was embarrassing.

Reverend McDonald held up a book. "This was written by the great scholar, Dr. W.E.B. DuBois," he said. "It is about the three great kingdoms of West Africa — Ghana, Mali, and Songhay."

It was exciting to know that Dr. DuBois had written a book about Africa. I had never heard of kingdoms in Africa. Far as I knew, Africa was a place where people ran around half naked with bones in their noses. But Reverend McDonald told us something different. Before slavery time, there were big cities in West Africa. They had large trading markets where gold and salt were traded. There were well-respected universities in places called Gao and Timbuktu. They even had libraries. Can you imagine that?

"And these were black people," said Reverend McDonald. "Yes, I said BLACK people." Erma flinched ever so slightly. "Don't hold your heads down, children. There is no shame in being black."

Mama hadn't intended to, but she stayed the entire time. And I saw a smile in her eyes that said she liked what she'd heard. So did I.

Monday, June 2, 1919

Rosie told us that most of the landlords who come to pick up rent on the first and second of every month are white men. But our landlord is a Colored man, Mr. John Brooks, one of the richest real estate men on the South Side. He's a nice enough person, but he is not like Mr. James or any of the others in the Colored Men's Improvement Association. There is nothing about Mr. Brooks that reminds me of any Colored man I know.

Tuesday, June 3, 1919

Rosie went South to visit her grandmother. She'll be gone until August. I will miss her. Sure wish I could see Grandma Nessie and Papa Till and Uncle John Willis. I'd even like to be bothered with my little cousins.

Mama's sewing machine arrived today! She was happy to see it as much as a long-time friend. She got busy stitching up things for us right away.

Mama said I looked "blue" all day. So we had fresh strawberries on cake tonight. Grandma Nessie was right. Chicago strawberries don't taste as good as the ones in Tennessee.

Wednesday, June 4, 1919

I wrote and asked Grandma Nessie again if it rained on Sundays May 25 and June 1.

Every day we learn a little more about the city. Mother Doris took Mama to a meeting of the Ida B. Wells Club last week, and she went again today. Mama has always admired Mrs. Wells-Barnett as one of the founders of the

NAACP. The women in her organization are working to put an end to lynching and to improve the lives of Colored women all over the nation.

Daddy has been working to get his funeral business going. He's found the perfect spot and even put down a deposit on the building. All that he needs now is a business license.

Thursday, June 5, 1919

Uncle Meese came by the apartment today. Funny he always comes to see us, but we never go to see him. Why? I didn't ask. Instead, Mr. Link stood by the car. I figured it was our chance to find out more about Uncle Meese's business.

"Where is Uncle Meese's office?" I asked.

"On Wabash Avenue."

"Do you help him do his work?" I asked.

"Yes."

Mr. Link was not very talkative today.

"And what part do you do?" I asked.

"I'm his driver and I'm the bouncer."

"What's a bouncer?"

"I throw people out of the club when they act up!"

Did Uncle Meese own a club? What kind of club? Was it like the NAACP or the women's clubs, but for men?

Erma wrote me:

I think it's a nightclub.
What is that?

Friday, June 6, 1919

On the way to the store, we met a Colored policeman. We've never seen a brown policeman before. Sheriff Bell is the only lawman in the Corners. Here there are policemen on every corner.

The one we met today told us his name is Big Wally. People call him that because he's very tall. He asked our names and asked if we were good little girls. We assured him that we were. "Good," he said, "because I would hate to have to put you in jail!"

Can you imagine me in jail? The idea of going to jail is awful. I like Big Wally.

>–⊹–◦–⊹–<

Saturday, June 7, 1919

We went to Reverend McDonald's lecture again today. He talked about violence. "There are all kinds of violence," he said. "Most people think its only violence when you beat, cut, or shoot another. But words can be violent weapons! Telling people they are stupid or ignorant is just as violent as hitting them."

Erma wrote to me:

I really liked what Reverend Prince said today. I know how words can be hurtful. They can hit you like a stone in the face. They can cut you like a hot knife. Words can be violent. But they can be loving and kind, too. It is how we use them. I want to use them to make people feel good the way Reverend Prince does.

When Erma writes about Reverend McDonald she calls him Reverend Prince. That name fits him perfectly. I will use it, too.

Monday, June 9, 1919

The *Crisis* came! Daddy didn't have to sneak and buy it. He read it to us from cover to cover, sharing articles, reading poems, and two good stories. Daddy doesn't have to hide the fact that he's a member of the NAACP anymore. Daddy has even joined the Chicago branch of the NAACP and has attended several meetings. The NAACP is going to hold a youth meeting and Erma and I are going.

Wednesday, June 11, 1919

Mama has joined the Ida B. Wells Club. She has met so many ladies from all over the neighborhood. Many of them from the South like us — Louisiana, Mississippi, Tennessee, Georgia, Kentucky, Texas, Alabama, and even Missouri. Almost every day a new family moves out and a new family moves in the next day.

Just yesterday the Martins moved out. A new family is moving in Friday. Their names are Ike and Mattie Phillips. We are disappointed that they don't have any children.

Thursday, June 12, 1919

We now know the address of Uncle Meese's club. We looked in Mama's address book and found out that it is located at 3319 Wabash. All we need to do now is find a way to get there. I can't wait to see the kind of club he owns.

Friday, June 13, 1919

Daddy came home from an NAACP meeting. He's real excited. The tenth anniversary of the NAACP will be celebrated at the annual conference in Cleveland. Daddy has been selected to attend the conference and to even make a speech about how difficult it is to be a member of the NAACP in the South.

He said he wasn't sure if he should go. "I should be using my time getting the business off the ground," he said. But Mama insisted that he should go to the conference. "People need to know what's going on," she said. "Go and tell your story and Pace's story."

We all could tell he really wanted to go to Cleveland, but Daddy needed to know that we wanted him to go as well.

Saturday, June 14, 1919

Instead of going to Reverend Prince's today, we went straight to the streetcar and used offering money to buy tickets. Erma held my trembling hand, and I thought two or three times to turn back, but we rode until we came to Wabash. Before long we found Uncle Meese's club.

We tried to sneak a look inside, but Mr. Link caught us! Then he hauled us into Uncle Meese's office.

"So you finally found out about your wayward uncle," he said. "I don't know why your mother thinks this is such an awful place. It is a well-respected supper club where people of quality come for good food and entertainment. There is no riffraff in here. Mr. Link sees to that. And this place has earned me a good and honest living. No wrong there, either."

Mama is so prim and proper at times. "She'd die if she knew we were here," I said. "But I just had to know what you did. Are you rich?"

"I am comfortable," said Uncle Meese. Then, hugging us both, he fetched Mr. Link to show us around and then take us home. "From now on," he added, "let me visit you."

Later

Erma wrote me:

I sure wanted to see Uncle Meese's club. Thanks for daring to go. I would have never had the nerve to go by myself. That's the good part about having a sister as curious as you are.

Wednesday, June 18, 1919

It has been a long and boring week. It has rained almost every day. Mama made us write letters. Erma wrote Aunt Thannie and I wrote Uncle Boston and Aunt Celia. I wanted to write William, but I've decided that I'm still mad at him. Mama writes him almost every week. He never writes back, though. What's wrong with that boy?

Thursday, June 19, 1919

It is a three-nineteen day again!

June is the sixth month! So I will add that to my numbers, 1 and 9 and 3.

$$6 \times 9 = 54 \text{ and } 5 + 4 = 9$$
$$3 \times 9 = 27 \text{ and } 7 + 2 = 9$$
$$9 \times 9 = 81 \text{ and } 8 + 1 = 9$$

Friday, June 20, 1919

Daddy came home very upset. The city rejected his application for a business license. They said his paperwork was not complete enough. I've never seen Daddy in such a state. Mama sent us to sit on the steps outside our apartment. But we heard everything anyway.

Daddy was ready to give up going to the NAACP meeting. But Mama knows how much it means to him to go.

"You can make a fresh start when you get back."

I'm glad he's still going.

Saturday, June 21, 1919

Daddy left for the NAACP conference in Cleveland, Ohio. He practiced his speech in front of us last night. He talked about the need to keep the *Crisis* available to people in the South, but in a way that was safe. He told how Mr. James put his life on the line to get copies to all the people who secretly belonged to the NAACP. Then he talked about increasing violence and suspicious deaths. When Daddy finished we applauded wildly.

"You will be the best speaker there," said Mama.

Daddy promised that he'd be home in time for the big Fourth of July celebration we've been reading about in the *Chicago Defender*.

Monday, June 23, 1919

Although our apartment is furnished, Mama has been busy putting her touch on things. We shopped at several nice stores along State Street. We didn't have to stand in the door and wait on somebody to allow us to come in, either. Chicago is noisy and smelly and busy all the time, but it's got a lot of good things to see and do.

Thursday, June 26, 1919

Erma and I turned down South Parkway and we knew that this was different from the other Colored neighborhoods we'd explored. We stopped before going on, because we thought we might have wandered into a white section. We didn't want to run into any Chicago Braxtons. When I looked closer I saw three Colored girls playing on the sidewalk.

I spoke to the girls.

"Who are you?" they asked.

"I'm Nell and this is Erma," I said.

"Nell and Erma, I am Amanda and these are my sisters — Hazie, short for Hazel, and Lonny, short for Yolanda Brooks. Do you live on this street?"

"No, we live at 2606 State Street," I said, happy to find possible playmates. Now that Rosie is gone, I have no one to talk to, and that gets lonely.

"Oh," said Amanda, who looked our age. She appeared to be disappointed. "And how long have you been in Chicago?"

"Just a month," I said.

"And where are you from: Alabama, Mississippi, or Kentucky?"

"Tennessee," I answered, not liking the tone of her voice.

"Figures. And where does your daddy work? The slaughterhouse or the train yard?"

"That's none of your business!" I said, hands on my hips. "Besides, what makes you think you're so much better off than we are?"

"Because we're not backward, Tennessee dirt tumblers, that's why." And Amanda and her sisters laughed and hurried away. Just when I was getting to like Chicago, I run into a girl who is just as bad as Billy Collins.

Later

Erma wrote me:

Amanda said her name is Brooks. *Our landlord's name is Brooks. Do you think she's his daughter?*

Friday, June 27, 1919

I got a letter from Grandma Nessie. She put my name on the envelope. It is a short letter, but just what I wanted to know.

> *My darling granddaughter:*
> *It rained on May 25th and on the 1st of June. So, at least for this year, it rained on Easter Sunday and on the seven Sundays thereafter. I miss you, darling.*
> *Love,*
> *Grandma Nessie*

Saturday, June 28, 1919

We went to the Open Mind Church and Youth Center today. Reverend Prince told us he had missed seeing us. He talked about thinking positively today. "Good things come from good thoughts," he said.

Erma wrote to me later:

> *I have a good thought. One day I will be a writer and I will write good thoughts.*

Sunday, June 29, 1919

Uncle Meese took us to a baseball game today. Two Colored teams played — the Chicago Giants and the Kansas City Monarchs. What an exciting game. The Giants won 11 to 4. Uncle Meese promised to take us again.

Monday, June 30, 1919

Daddy got home today from the NAACP meeting. He wanted to tell us everything, but he couldn't all at once. Slowly we heard it piece by piece. First, his speech went well. Mama was excited to hear about Mrs. Ida B. Wells-Barnett's speech, too. It was about how important it is to keep up the work to get anti-lynching laws passed.

But the best part was when Daddy told us about meeting and shaking the hands of Dr. DuBois and James Weldon Johnson.

Daddy brought Erma and me each a book of poems by a poet named Fenton Johnson. My book is *Songs of the Soil*, and Erma Jean's is *Visions of Dusk*. I am trying to memorize one of his poems.

Erma's favorite poem is one titled "Tired." I read it to her three times.

Wednesday, July 2, 1919

The Phillipses went back to Memphis. They hadn't lasted a month. A new couple just moved in, Mr. and Mrs. Smalls.

There was a terrible thunderstorm. Mama came and sat by us. She didn't have to say anything. But her being beside us made me feel better.

Thursday, July 3, 1919

Daddy and Uncle Meese had words today. Uncle Meese wants to help Daddy get his business license. "I will not do it your way," Daddy said.

"You'll never get a license *without* doing it my way," said Uncle Meese.

"Yes, I will," Daddy insisted.

What was that about? I wondered out loud.

Erma wrote to me:

Uncle Meese wants Daddy to pay a bribe to get his license.

Daddy would never do that.

Friday, July 4, 1919

There was a parade down State Street today. We stood in the window and watched it pass. Flags waving, bands marching. It was better than any one I could remember down home. Mr. Williams bar-be-qued in a big tin tub out on the sidewalk. The smell was so familiar and wonderful.

Daddy wasn't happy. "That's what gives us newcomers a bad name," he said. "We need to put all those country ways behind us. Stop bar-be-queing in tin tubs on the front!" He stormed into the bedroom with his copy of the *Crisis* and closed the door. I didn't care what Mr. Williams bar-be-qued in. It was delicious.

Monday, July 7, 1919

We got a letter from Grandma Nessie and Papa Till. They said they were all well. The Klan had burned down Mr. James's barbershop and left a burning cross in his yard. They almost burned his house, but Sheriff Bell called them off. I thought of Josie and how scared she must have been. I wrote her a letter. I'm so glad we are not down there!

Tuesday, July 8, 1919

We heard somebody hollering, screaming on the first floor. We all came running, thinking the worst had happened to somebody. It was Miz Hamilton jumping from foot to foot, holding a piece of paper. "I've been accepted," she said. "I've been accepted in the Madam C.J. Walker Beauty School. I start classes next week."

I know about Madam C.J. Walker from the *Crisis*. She was the first Colored woman to earn a million dollars. She manufactured hair and skin care products. She made one cream that lightens your skin. Erma begged for some when she first saw it advertised, but Mama wouldn't let her have it. "Live in the skin you are in."

Erma had been saving up her money so she could buy a jar of the bleaching cream. I asked if she was still interested.

She wrote me:

NO!

This is another good thing about Chicago. Living here has made a big difference in Erma. We have Reverend Prince to thank for that change in her.

Thursday, July 10, 1919

Daddy is busy getting all the paperwork for his funeral parlor together. He goes downtown early in the morning and he doesn't come back until late in the evening. The owner of the building Daddy put the deposit down on said he will only hold the building one more week.

Tuesday, July 15, 1919

We decided to explore more of our neighborhood today. Before we realized it, we had wandered to the stockyards. Suddenly, five or six white boys jumped out from behind a sidetracked train car. They surrounded us. "Where you going?" they asked. They poked at us. Pulled our hair. We ran as fast as we could, but not before I recognized one of the boys. Can you believe it? It was Tommy Braxton.

When I told Mama that I had seen Tommy Braxton she clicked her teeth and shook her head. "Lord have mercy," she said. "They must have come here after the tornado. I guess whites are coming to Chicago for the same reasons we are — better jobs, better pay, better education."

That scares me so bad! If people like the Braxtons come to Chicago, it will soon be as bad as it is in the South.

Friday, July 18, 1919

It was so hot last night. Too hot to sleep. I don't remember feeling that hot in Tennessee — ever! Daddy told us to get a quilt, and we all got on the streetcar and went to 26th Street and walked to the beach along Lake Michigan. The sand was warm beneath our toes. I have to admit it felt every bit as good as Tennessee river mud.

We laid out our quilts and lay on our backs, looking up at the stars. I found all the stars that Uncle Pace had taught me to find — Pegasus, the Big Dipper, Hercules, and Orion. The wind off the lake felt so cool and soothing to our dry skin. Mama told stories about when she was a girl, and Daddy recited from memory the story of creation from Genesis. It was so beautiful – Daddy's big voice under a star-studded tent.

We lay there on the beach until the sky began to lighten. Then we gathered our things and came home. Home. It's the first time I have called Chicago home.

Saturday, July 19, 1919

It's another three-nineteen day.
91
19

91
19
91
19 = 330
I just looked at the clock and it is 3:30.

There are about twenty-five of us now in Reverend Prince's lecture class. It is growing. He talked today about colors. "Red is a happy color. Yellow is a warm color. Blue is a cool color. What do you feel when I say black? Black makes some people feel sad."

He asked us to raise our hands if black made us feel bad. Erma raised her hand slowly. I raised mine.

"Black is a wonderful color. Think of all the good things that are black," said Reverend Prince.

Erma's list:
Good black things are . . .
Mama's gloves
My winter coat
My good shoes
My favorite comb
My sister's eyes
My hair
Me

My list:
Good black things are . . .
Coal
Storm clouds
Rich growing soil
Night
My eyes
Blackberries
*My teeth after eating
    blackberries*

I was so surprised when Erma wrote herself. She said she was black. I can't believe she did that. Back home she would have never done that.

Our lists made Reverend Prince very happy. "Is there anything *bad* or *wrong* on your lists?"

We all said no. I think I answered the loudest. No, Reverend Prince is not a charlatan.

Monday, July 21, 1919

Uncle Meese came to visit again. He and Daddy have agreed to disagree. He was overjoyed because a horse named Sir Barton had won a horse race. Daddy sent us to the steps, but we heard it all anyway.

"Not just any horse race," said Uncle Meese. "This was the Triple Crown at the Belmont Stakes. No horse has ever won the Kentucky Derby, the Preakness, and the Belmont Stakes. The odds were against that he'd do it. But Sir Barton brought home the bacon. I made it big, and I'm willing to share." But Daddy said he didn't want any part of gambling money.

I would love to see a horse race, almost as much as I'd like to go inside Uncle Meese's club when it's open — with people in it, and entertainers singing and dancing.

Mama would faint dead away if she knew I was even thinking such a thought.

Tuesday, July 22, 1919

Daddy came home today feeling very, very bad. He didn't get his license for a second time. "They've run me ragged," he said, rubbing his temples. "I did everything they asked me to do. Still it isn't enough. They want more. I think if I slip a few dollars under the table. . . ."

Mama would not hear of it! "Never!" she said. "It isn't right."

Later

Mama sent us down to Mother Doris's because she and Daddy had somewhere to go.

I wonder what is going to become of us if Daddy can't get his business going? Will we have to go back to Tennessee?

>-·-‹›-·-O-·-‹›-·-‹

Wednesday, July 23, 1919

Mama and Daddy went to see a lawyer yesterday. One of Uncle Meese's friends. Maybe he will help Daddy get a license.

It is so hot, Erma and I don't feel like talking or walking. Mama taught us how to fold a fan using paper. Then, to keep ourselves occupied while she sewed, we decorated our fans with colors. I put a daisy on mine. Erma put a rose on hers. After dinner we sat in the window and fanned, using our homemade fans.

Thursday, July 24, 1919

We got a letter from Grandma Nessie and Papa Till. They hoped we are well. They said the weather was hot and dry. And that other than a touch of arthritis both of them were "steppin', if not too high." They reported that Uncle John Willis had cut his hand, but Dr. Shipp had stitched it up as good as new. Uncle Boston and Celia had a new baby girl whose name is Honesta June Love. They asked about the business and how it was going. Then they sent love to all of us.

Daddy's business? He hasn't told them what's going on here.

Friday, July 25, 1919

Daddy is like a big soap bubble. If the slightest thing touches him, I think he will just pop. "What's a man to do? I've lost the place I had picked out for my funeral home, and the deposit! Now the lawyer I hired to help me says there's nothing he can do! Wants me to pay the bribe." Daddy sounds so discouraged, but Mama won't let him give up or give in to the pressure to pay a bribe. "There's one more person I'm going to call on," he said. "After that, then I'll have to consider what we are to do next."

Later

Daddy had Mama dress us in our best clothes and together we all went to see Mr. Hill, the man we met on the train, at the Colored bank. A Colored banker was something to see.

Daddy was as nervous as a cat stepping over hot tar. He had made an appointment for 1:00 in the afternoon, but we were dressed and ready at noon. "I want you to be on your best behavior," said Daddy. "Speak when you are spoken to and not before." He was talking directly to me, because Erma can't talk.

Daddy told Mr. Hill how he had tried to get a license to open his funeral home. "I've been denied three times. I refuse to pass money under the table. And I was wondering if there isn't something that can be done," said Daddy.

Mr. Hill leaned back in his chair. "It's also the reality of the city," he said. Then, after thinking for a moment, Mr. Hill sat forward again. "We need more of your kind of people here in Chicago," he said. "You have a lovely family." Mr. Hill began to write. "Here is an introductory letter to Mr. Robert Abbott, a very good friend of mine. We arrived here in Chicago at about the same time. He's now the owner and editor of the *Chicago Defender*. This letter will get you in to him. And if anybody can help you here in Chicago, it is Robert Abbott."

I haven't seen Daddy look so relieved since we arrived in Chicago. Maybe I was wrong about Mr. Hill being a Colored "uppity-class" snob. He helped Daddy and I'm grateful.

Saturday, July 26, 1919

Guess who came home today! William. William is home! Can you imagine?

Uncle Meese knocked on the door first. When I answered, Uncle Meese stepped aside and there stood

William. Except for being a little thin, he is as handsome as ever.

William got discharged from the army early. "They didn't need me and besides, I was underage," he said biting into a piece of Mama's jelly cake.

So he had gotten a job washing dishes and saved his money. Then he borrowed the rest from Aunt Thannie for a train ticket.

I was cool toward William. At first he tried teasing, but I wouldn't let him charm me. We sat on the steps and talked for a while.

"It's so sad seeing Erma like that — silent. So sad!"

"You should have come home for Uncle Pace's funeral. We needed you," I said. "Poor Erma needed you. I needed you. And you didn't come. You didn't write! Now you show up, when everything is fine."

William didn't answer me for the longest time. "Nellie Lee," he said.

"Call me Nell. Nellie Lee is country-sounding. It's hard being called 'backward' and 'country bumpkins' because we talk slower and have double names."

"I know 'bout that," he said. "I sure got teased about saying things like 'commenced' and 'reckon' and 'y'all'."

William was quiet for a spell. Then, when he spoke again, he was very serious, as if he was speaking out of another part of himself — a part he didn't let too many people hear.

"Nell," he said, "you are right. I was wrong, but the truth is I have not been able to come home. They have been lynching black men like swatting flies. I was just plain scared. And that's the truth."

"You could have written."

"You know me and pencils have never made friends."

We sat quietly. It felt good to have my brother home. "What'd you bring me?" I asked at last.

"Me!" he said, laughing.

I decided that was good enough. But I didn't tell him that.

Sunday, July 27, 1919

To celebrate William's homecoming, we decided to go to the beach. Mama made some of her good fried chicken. We haven't seen Daddy so lively since he'd returned from the NAACP meeting in Cleveland. Then the day went sour like milk too long in the sun.

Whites swim at the 29th Street beach and Coloreds swim at the 26th Street beach. Our neighbors Mr. and Mrs. Williams and Eugene joined us.

We were all splashing in the water when we looked out

and saw Eugene floating on a railroad tie. I waved at him, and he waved back. Suddenly, we heard people yelling at him to turn back. I guess Eugene didn't notice that he had drifted across the invisible line into the white section.

When Eugene realized what was happening, it was too late. Five or six white men paddled out. Eugene tried to swim away, but the crowd began to call him names and throw rocks. Then the Colored bathers began to hurl rocks too. Daddy saw what was happening and he ordered us out of the water. He didn't intend to have to say it again.

Soaking wet, we grabbed up our things. I kept looking back, but Daddy was forcing us to hurry. The Colored people were upset and beginning to gather to see what was going on. We couldn't find William or Uncle Meese anywhere. But as we rushed across the street, we saw two Colored policemen running toward the beach. One was Big Wally. Somebody screamed. It sounded like Mrs. Williams. "He's drowning. Somebody help him."

This can't be happening. Not in Chicago. This isn't Alabama, Mississippi, Georgia . . . or Tennessee!

>-!-+>-O-<+-!-<

Monday, July 28, 1919

I thought when we came to Chicago we would not see any more horrible things happening to people because of the color of their skin. But we are right in the middle of a race riot. It's hard to describe what is going on. The white newspapers say that Colored people started the riot at the beach. The *Defender* newspaper says the riot started because whites were the cause of Eugene Williams' drowning and they did nothing to save him. When the police came, the Colored people told what happened to Eugene and pointed out those who had chased him into deep water and thrown rocks. The police refused to arrest anyone, arguing that it was just an accident. A shot was fired and in the end Big Wally was killed.

Eugene is dead. Big Wally is, too. And people are fighting in the streets. But this riot is not like the ones we have read about. Here in Chicago, Colored people are fighting back.

Tuesday, July 29, 1919

During the day, things are not so bad, but as soon as the whistle blows at the stockyard, it starts all over again. The rock throwing, the shooting, the beatings.

Reverend Prince came to our apartment earlier today and asked if he might store his picture of the Black Jesus here. "I have no family in Chicago," he said. "And if anything should happen to me, I can't think of anybody I'd rather have this than my star pupils, Nell and Erma."

Daddy allowed that he would be happy to keep it. Daddy invited Reverend Prince to stay with us, but he went back to be with those who came to his church because they had no families, either. "Ignorance and fear breed violence," he said. "Knowledge is the only way to overcome intolerance. So, I've got to go back into the streets and try to do what I can to stop this nightmare."

We pray that he will not be hurt.

Later That Same Afternoon

Mama is upstairs sitting with Mr. and Mrs. Williams. We are with Mother Doris. Two Cat got out, and poor Mother Doris is so disturbed. Erma was taking a nap. I figured Two Cat couldn't be far, so, without thinking, I went out looking for her.

I didn't realize how far I must have strayed from the house. Suddenly, I heard a gang of white boys coming across the street ahead of me. They were carrying baseball bats and rocks and calling out challenges. I heard shattering glass. My feet seemed bolted to the ground. I closed my eyes not knowing what to expect. Then someone pulled me into a basement doorway. It was Tommy Braxton. He covered my mouth to keep me from screaming.

"Hush!" he said as the yelling gang went past. When it was safe, he let me go. "You could get killed out here, girl," he said.

"What's the matter with you, Tommy Braxton? You help and hurt at the same time. You're mixed up in the head! And I don't know what to think of you." Tommy took me by the arm and led me between two buildings, and by using shortcuts he led me safely back to my front door.

"Pa says we're poor, but at least we ain't Colored," Tommy explained. "But your family was always nice to my mama — I can't forget that. . . . Now I've paid you back. I don't owe you no more. Get in your house and stay there. If you get caught, I can't help you."

Two Cat was sitting on the stoop, licking her paws, and looking unconcerned about the world around her. I scooped her up and hurried back into the house just as someone called, "Hey, is that you, Braxton? Where have you been?" Mother Doris never realized that I had gone out and come back in.

Later That Same Night

Mama is worried sick about William and what might have happened to him. Uncle Meese knows his way around, so I'm not too worried about him. But William has only been in Chicago two days and now he's caught up in a riot.

Somebody hurled a rock through Miz Hamilton's window, and she ran up to our apartment. We all huddled together listening to the gunshots and screams.

Poor Erma whimpered softly in Mama's arms. I held on to Mama's other arm. The air was thick with fear and worry. Without warning, Daddy leaped to his feet. "I'm not going to cower here in the darkness while a mob of hate-mongers holds me captive in my own house!"

"What are you doing, Freeman?" Mama's voice was shaking.

"I'm going out there," he said, "to fight for my neighborhood. And if I die, then let me go down trying to defend my family."

Mama begged him not to go. Miz Hamilton pleaded with him to be reasonable. I was crying. Then deep from within Erma came a scream that stopped us all in our tracks. And for the first time since February, Erma Jean Love spoke words. "No, Daddy, no! Don't go out there! They will kill you the way they did Uncle Pace!"

Later

Daddy didn't go. Instead, we sat in the darkness as Erma told us what had happened to Uncle Pace. Here is the story as Erma told it to us:

> The night he died, Uncle Pace told me
> what happened. He wanted us to know that
> he wasn't drunk, and he hadn't been hit by a
> train, either. He took the local from Nashville
> to the Corners. There were no seats in the
> Colored car, so he sat in the whites only
> coach. When he reached the Corners, sev-
> eral men got off with him. They beat him
> with sticks and rocks. Then they poured
> whiskey on him and left him on the tracks,
> but he managed to pull himself off the tracks
> before the train moved. The men who did it
> got back on the train and went on their way.

It was like losing Uncle Pace all over again. But it was so good hearing Erma's voice again. When she had fin-ished, Mama and Daddy and I smothered her with hugs and kisses. In the midst of all the smashing windows, gunshots, and shouting, our family has something to be thankful for.

Wednesday, July 30, 1919

Still no word of William. Mama is so worried about him. The whole time he was in the army, she didn't worry like this. He was last seen with Uncle Meese, so we're hoping they are still together.

Our food is running short. Mama found a few cookies and we divided them. When Daddy could stand it no longer, he decided to go looking for William and to get food.

Thunder is rumbling in the distance. Daddy taught me that if I count the seconds between the flash of lightning and when we hear the thunder, then each second is a mile.

Lightning flashed. 1001, 1002, 1003, 1004, 1005. Low thunder rumblings. That means the storm is five miles away. Maybe Daddy will get back before it gets too bad.

Later

Daddy returned just before the downpour. He had food but no news about William or Uncle Meese.

Before Dawn, Thursday, July 31, 1919

Usually, a knock in the middle of the night means bad news, but not this morning. Dr. Kebbs from upstairs stopped by the apartment. He brought us a message from Uncle Meese. "Your brother and son are fine," he reassured Daddy. "He is at Provident with his friend Mr. Link who was hurt, but he will survive."

Poor Doc Kebbs looked so tired. He said he had been working since the beginning of the riots.

What a relief to know William is fine.

Later That Day

Mercifully, rain has come and cooled off both the weather and tempers. Mayor Thompson has called out the militia to patrol the streets and stop the riot. Slowly, people are beginning to come out of their apartments after days of being penned in.

William and Uncle Meese came to the house. Such hugging and tears — especially when they heard that Erma could talk again, and had told Uncle Pace's story. "I knew something like that must have happened," said William.

Uncle Meese said that he and William had narrowly

escaped when his car was attacked by a mob. Mr. Link fought them off and sped away, but not before he was wounded in the arm.

Later That Same Night

"What do you think of Chicago now?" I just asked Erma.

She picked up her book to write, then remembered she could talk. She smiled and decided she would rather write her thoughts anyway.

She wrote:

Chicago, wild and terrible Chicago.
You scare me.
You make me want to run and hide.
Chicago, awful, smelly Chicago.
You aren't Tennessee.
You aren't the Corners.
You are bigger, meaner, and
You scare me.

Erma is right. Chicago is in many ways no better than the South. Here there are people who hurt and hate, too. I am so disappointed.

Friday, August 1, 1919

The rioting isn't as bad, but it hasn't stopped. . . . It is still going on. So Mama will not let us go outside the apartment building. It is hot and muggy and we are all ready to scream!

Daddy wrote and told all the family how Uncle Pace died. He also wrote a letter to Sheriff Bell, telling him what happened. "I don't expect anything to come of it, but at least they will stop saying Pace was drunk and got hit by a train."

Sunday, August 3, 1919

Mama is upstairs sitting with Mrs. Williams who is heartsick over Eugene. Daddy and other members of the NAACP went with Mr. Williams to the coroner's jury. It was ruled that Eugene had drowned from "fear."

Reports of that decision set off another wave of fighting and violence through the city. Won't it ever end? Will there ever be a time when people stop hating and hurting one another?

>-+>-O-<+-<

Saturday, August 9, 1919

Mama, Daddy, and I returned the Black Jesus to Reverend Prince today. He was overjoyed to have it back, and we were glad he was doing so well himself. Erma thanked him for being so kind to her while she was afflicted. His basement meeting hall was damaged, but he and his members are helping to repair it.

He offered to pay Erma and me to help sweep. We did it for free.

Thursday, August 14, 1919

The *Crisis* came today. Daddy read to us as usual. Then he read the *Defender*. It says that over thirty-eight people were killed here in Chicago — fifteen white and twenty-three Colored. Hundreds and hundreds of people have been hurt or had their property damaged. The riots will not likely be forgotten by anybody who lived through them. White people rarely come into our neighborhood anymore. And we dare not go beyond the South Side — especially after dark.

I told Erma about how Tommy Braxton saved my life. She fussed at me about being outside during the riots anyway, but then she made me tell her every single detail about what had happened.

Friday, August 15, 1919

Mr. Brooks, our landlord, came over to see the damage done to his apartment building. He brought along Amanda. We hadn't seen her since we'd met on the street. Erma and I jumped rope and pretended not to notice her. "Aren't you concerned about getting hot and sweaty?" she asked. "And smelly, too. Ugh!"

"That's what water is for," Erma said.

"When we get hot and sweaty, we take a bath," I said. "What about you?"

That shut up Miss Muffet.

"Thought you couldn't talk," Amanda said to Erma.

"The Devil thought the turkey couldn't fly but it did!" Erma answered.

"Where'd you get *that* old country saying?"

"I'd rather be country and nice than citified."

It feels so good having my sister back with me. It took one bad thing to take her voice; it took another to get it back. Now she's whole again.

Tuesday, August 19, 1919

It is a three-nineteen day. Everything seems to be 19 cents more than what it is worth. Food prices have gone sky high. Mama complained at the meat market that the meat was not fresh, yet the prices were far too high. "Take it or leave it," the clerk said. Mama left it.

Wednesday, August 20, 1919

Mr. and Mrs. Williams went back South today. They didn't even give a month's notice. Losing Eugene was more than Mrs. Williams could stand. "At least at home, we got family," she said.

Friday, August 22, 1919

With all that's been going on, Daddy just now got an appointment with Mr. Robert Abbott, the editor of the *Defender*. Mr. Hill's letter helped make it possible.

When Daddy came home, his spirits were somewhat lifted. The meeting had been short, but Mr. Abbott had promised to help.

Tuesday, August 26, 1919

In the meantime, Mr. Abbott suggested that Daddy take a job so he would appear more stable. So Daddy took a job as a porter at the McKinley Music Publishing Company on East 55th Street.

Food has gotten even more expensive and Mr. Brooks has gone up on our rent a whole quarter — even though he didn't have to replace but one window.

William is staying full time with Uncle Meese. Mama doesn't like it because of the "surroundings."

Mama has no idea that we know about Uncle Meese's supper club. It tickles us when Mama and Daddy try to talk over our heads, spelling words.

Wednesday, August 27, 1919

Mama attended an anti-lynching rally with her women's Club members. A mob tried to break them up, but the ladies locked arms and stood their ground. Some white ladies joined them, and the mob backed down. It was a small victory for the anti-lynching movement, but it was a big one for Mama. I could just imagine Mama carrying an anti-lynching sign, wearing white gloves, a hat, and a pocketbook. Even while protesting, Mama is bound to be a lady.

"I was scared to death," Mama said when she told us the story. "But when those rowdies came, I didn't care about my personal safety. I was ready to go down, standing up for my rights. Lynching has to stop!"

Daddy was proud of Mama, but he was concerned. "I don't think you should protest anymore," he said.

Mama sent us into the hallway where we sat on the steps and listened to the rest of their argument. "Freeman," she said. "I will never give up my work with the anti-lynching movement — not for you, not for anybody. And furthermore, I'm going to join the Alpha Sufferage Club Mrs. Wells-Barnett helped to start. We women aim to get the right to vote."

For the first time in our lives our father was speechless. Erma and I cheered for Mama. "I hear you out there, girls," he said. I guess he heard us giggle, too.

Thursday, August 28, 1919

Daddy has never had to work for anybody in his life except Papa Till. He doesn't like it. And I think I understand how the sharecroppers feel. No matter how hard Daddy works, his pay is low.

Friday, August 29, 1919

Rosie's home and it's her birthday. Her hair is beautiful. Like magic, all the kinks are gone and her hair is glossy and smooth. "Mama fixed it for my birthday," she said.

What did Rosie mean by "fixed it"? How do you fix hair?

Miz Hamilton and Mama took us to the park where we ran and played for hours. Since the riots, Mama has not let us leave the front of the house without being with her or Daddy. I loved running with the wind against my face. It was the first time in weeks that I felt that everything might be fine. I sure would like to go swimming, but we haven't been near the lake since the riots. Rosie said she didn't want to go swimming anyway, because she didn't want her hair to "go back."

Go back where? Rosie explained the phrase meant her hair would return (go back) to being kinky again. Strange!

Anyway, we told Rosie everything that has happened and she hung on very word. We told her about Erma getting her voice back. We had so much fun, we didn't mind getting sweaty one bit. On the way home we bought penny suckers and we licked on them until our tongues were sore. It was a good day.

Saturday, August 30, 1919

With the help of a lot of people, Reverend Prince has put his basement room back in order better than before. Our Saturday meetings started again today. William took us, because Mama still won't trust us out of her sight alone.

Reverend Prince talked about Africa again. "Yes," he said. "Africa *is* a dark continent. It is filled with dark — very dark — people. And that's not a bad thing. One day we will return to Africa and be welcomed by our lost families. But we're not ready yet. When we can say with pride that we are descendents of BLACK Africans, maybe then we will be able to make that journey back home."

"I like Reverend Prince," said William. He promised to take us anytime we wanted. But he's applied for a job as a Pullman car porter. If he gets it, he'll be off and gone again.

I guess William can't help it. He's like a rolling stone.

Later

While we had William to ourselves, Erma and I asked him to tell us about Uncle Meese's club. "Who goes there? What do they do inside?"

William laughed. "Does Mama know *you* know about Uncle Meese's club?"

"No," said Erma. "But do tell us about it, please!"

William painted a wonderful word picture of Uncle Meese's club. "It isn't a tavern or a juke joint, no," he said. "It's a high-class nightclub where people come and they are entertained by some of the best musicians in the business! Nothing vulgar or low-life about it," he added. "Uncle Meese is all class."

"Mama and Daddy are so old-fashioned," I said.

"Mama gets scandalized when somebody wears red to church on Sunday!" Erma put in, laughing.

William was really surprised when we told him how Mama had joined the suffrage movement and the anti-lynching league.

"Our Mama?"

"Our Mama!"

"Can you imagine that?"

Monday, September 1, 1919

Mama took us to register for school today. School was scheduled to start this week, but classes won't start until next week because of the riots. Just think, in the Corners school would be letting out for the fall harvest.

I have never been in a school as large as Dunbar. Our little one-room school in the Corners with the leaky roof would have fit in the center hallway of Dunbar. And there's not just one teacher but lots of them — and a principal who does nothing but principal.

They said they had to give us tests to see which grades we will be in. Back in the Corners we had two levels — elementary and intermediate. That was it.

The woman who gave us the tests said at age eleven I am supposed to be in fourth grade. And at age twelve, Erma is supposed to be in fifth grade. Rosie is ten, so she is supposed to be in third grade. But we have to be tested to see where we will be placed.

The test was HARD! I've never heard of some of the words on the test. Like they asked, What is an iron horse? I had no idea.

Tuesday, September 2, 1919

William left for St. Louis. Got the job! It was hard to see him leave us again. But William is restless and running on the railroad will be good for him.

>─┤◄►─O─◄►┤─◄

Thursday, September 4, 1919

Uncle Meese stopped by the house to say good-bye. He was on his way to Harlem to visit with Thannie and then on to Paris, France, for a vacation. He offered to let Daddy run the club but Mama was not happy. So Mr. Link will be in charge until Uncle Meese returns. Before leaving, Uncle Meese tried to give Daddy money to pay the bribe in order to get his license. But Daddy still wouldn't agree to that. "Well, at least use my automobile while I'm away," Uncle Meese said, giving Daddy his keys.

Chicago will not be the same without William or Uncle Meese. But at least William is a lot closer to home than Paris, France.

Friday, September 5, 1919

We got a letter today from the Chicago Board of Education. It said that I tested at third grade. Erma did not make fifth or fourth grade. So she has been assigned to Miss Franklin's third grade, too.

Erma Jean hates the idea of being in the same class with me. She has always been ahead of me. She felt a little bit better when she found out that Rosie was put in second grade.

Later

Miz Hamilton finished the Madam C. J. Walker Beauty School course yesterday. She got a certificate saying she can fix hair and sell products made by Madam Walker. Mama made an appointment for her to "fix" our hair.

First she washed mine with a shampoo that smelled good enough to eat.

"You've got good hair," Miz Hamilton said, drying it with a towel. "Long, thick, and straight." Then, turning to Erma, she said, "Now, honey, you got some bad hair. But not to worry, I can fix it up so people will think you've got white folks' hair."

That made me boil on the inside, but I kept my mouth shut. Miz Hamilton is a nice person. She meant no harm, but she was sounding just like those Colored people who think the only way to be pretty is to look white. The only way to have good hair is for it to be straight.

Miz Hamilton pressed Erma's hair with a hot comb. Actually, it was like magic. All the kinks melted away and Erma's hair was straight, glossy, and smooth.

"Now my hair is as pretty as yours," Erma said, smiling. The smile on her face was glowing. She liked the way her hair looked.

"It always was pretty," I answered.

Monday, September 8, 1919

Today was the first day of school. Erma and I wore blue skirts and white blouses that Mama had made. We felt so special when Daddy drove us up to the school in Uncle Meese's pretty motorcar — just ahead of Amanda Brooks. Nobody needed to know that the motorcar wasn't ours. All eyes were on us as we strutted up the front steps and into the building. We certainly didn't look like country bumpkins!

There are forty-three children in our class. All of them are Colored. Miss Franklin is Colored, but there are white teachers and our principal is white. That could never be in the Corners.

There weren't enough desks for us all, or enough books, either. Miss Franklin said we are to get more desks later on in the week.

Miss Franklin is nice and she's pretty, too. I've got a feeling she won't be a teacher long. Somebody is sure to marry her.

>─┼─◇─○─◇─┼─◁

Tuesday, September 9, 1919

We walked to school this morning, and that was fine. All we needed was for somebody like Amanda Brooks to see us in a motorcar once. Nobody teased us. But they sure tease the children who have double names and wear overalls and don't comb their hair. Erma and I didn't poke fun at anybody, but we didn't try to shame the teasers out of it, either. We were scared they would turn on us. So we kept our mouths shut.

Wednesday, September 10, 1919

We got more school desks, but they sure aren't new. Uncle John Willis made all the desks at our school down home. They were solid, well-built. They were about the only things solid in that old falling-down school. This is a big fine school, but these old desks are falling apart. Wouldn't it be nice if we could get Uncle John Willis to make the desks for up here? Then we would have a good school and good desks all in the same place.

There are five rows across with eight desks deep. The teacher's desk is surrounded by our desks. It reminds me of the way cotton grows all the way around the sharecropper's house — right up to the front door.

Ever since the placement test, I've been wondering what an iron horse is. Erma said it was a statue. So I finally got a chance to ask Miss Franklin. "The three choices were a locomotive, a blacksmith's anvil, or a statue. I guessed it was a locomotive."

"You guessed correctly," said Miss Hamilton.

Funny. I don't feel any smarter because I know the answer.

Thursday, September 11, 1919

I knew it was too good to be true. Nobody had teased us about being Southern. We didn't talk slow and split our verbs. We were clean and our hair was combed and we even wore ribbons. And we made sure nobody called us by two names. But all Amanda was waiting for was a reason to get on to us. And sure enough she did.

"Where did you two get those Mammy-made dresses?" she asked. Mama has always made our clothes. She refuses to buy clothes that we can't try on. So she makes them for us. Next to what the other children wore in the Corners, our dresses looked like something princesses would wear. But here in Chicago, they look — well, Mammy-made!

To make matters worse, a woman from the health department came and passed out free soap. "Make sure you use it," Amanda said before she strutted off to get in her motorcar.

I do not like that girl!

Friday, September 12, 1919

Mama came to the school with Erma Jean and me. She put the soap on Miss Franklin's desk and said in a soft and polite way, "We have plenty of soap at home and we use it regularly."

Miss Franklin accepted it back graciously. "I will pass the soap on to someone who needs it more," she said. And that was that. When Miss Franklin opened her desk there were at least ten bars of soap other people had returned. She and Mama laughed at the same time.

Monday, September 15, 1919

The weekend went by so fast. Nothing special happened.

Now I understand why they were passing out soap last week. Some of the people who brought it back should have kept it. A number of children come to school looking like they haven't seen water in weeks.

You'll never guess who I saw at school today! Bud Simmons, our coal man from the Corners. I was glad until I looked at him — really looked at him. His clothing was dirty and he smelled awful. His hair was uncombed and his teeth were rotten in front. Alice Mary, his daughter, didn't look any better. I hate to say it, but I was ashamed of them! I hurried away without even asking about Papa Till and Grandma Nessie.

Now I am angry with myself for being ashamed of people I've known all my life. When I told Mama, she said, "The big city has a way of making us forget where we've come from. Don't ever fall into that trap of thinking you're better off that somebody because you've got stuff and things. It is better to act beautiful than to be beautiful. And it is far better to be smart than to act smart."

Tomorrow I will find Alice Mary Simmons and do the right thing.

Tuesday, September 16, 1919

We sang the Negro National Anthem, "Lift Ev'ry Voice and Sing," today. Miss Franklin was surprised that Erma and I knew it. Daddy taught it to us and told us the story of how James Weldon Johnson and Rosamond Johnson had written the words and music in 1900. We were not allowed to sing the song in school back home. Some kids from Alabama and Mississippi had never even heard it before. When the teacher asked me how I knew so much about James Weldon Johnson, I was afraid to answer. Would Daddy get into trouble if I told Miss Franklin he is a member of the NAACP and that he reads the *Crisis* to us? I couldn't take any chances, so I just shrugged my shoulders and sat down.

I found Alice Mary Simmons and walked part of the way home with her. We are the same age, but she got put back with Rosie. I asked Rosie to look after her for me. Rosie fussed about it a little. "That girl is coun-*try*," she said. "But I'll do it for you."

Alice Mary must have used some of the soap, because she looked a little bit cleaner than she did yesterday.

Erma and I invited her to go with us to the Saturday meeting at the Open Mind Church and Youth Center. She seemed so happy just being with people she knew.

Friday, September 19, 1919

Another three-nineteen day. But this time the month is 9 also.

So it's

9 - 19 - 1919

9 + 19 = 28

9 + 19 = 28

$$9 + 19 = 28$$
$$19 + 28 + 28 = 75$$
$$7 + 5 = 12 \text{ --- Erma's age}$$

Saturday, September 20, 1919

Alice Mary enjoyed the meeting with Reverend Prince.

The topic today was about doing things because it makes you feel better, not because you're trying to prove something to somebody. "Do the right thing for the right reasons," said Reverend Prince. "Clean yourself up because it is the healthy and wholesome thing to do, not because you're trying to appear better off than a neighbor who is less fortunate. Educate yourself because you want to know, not to prove you are as smart as a person of some other race. Walk with your head up because you like looking your neighbor straight in the face and not down your nose at him."

Soap and water clean the flesh.
Truth scrubs the mind.

Erma wrote in her diary, too. But she's not sharing her diary with me anymore. "I'm able to talk now," she said.

"So my diary is private again. Promise you won't sneak and read it!"

Promise!

Monday, September 22, 1919

Alice Mary came to school clean today. I told Daddy about how the children were teasing her so badly, the way they had teased us when we first came. So, he did something real special. He asked Mr. Link to drive us along with Alice Mary to school today, which he did! I thought Amanda and all the other uppity girls would drop their teeth when they saw Mr. Link chauffeuring us right up to the front door!

Everybody started looking at Alice Mary a little differently, as I knew they would. Couldn't help but think about what Reverend Prince had said about doing right things for the right reasons. For whatever reason, I loved it!

Tuesday, September 23, 1919

It has been a while, but Mr. Abbott sent a letter to Daddy saying that he had spoken to Mr. Oscar DePriest, the first black city alderman, about his case. Mr. DePriest has agreed to meet with Daddy.

Maybe it won't be long now until Daddy gets his license — and without having to pay a bribe.

Tuesday, September 30, 1919

I asked Miss Franklin if we would be studying anything about the great cities in Africa that had a library and a university. She laughed and said there was no such place. I told her that Reverend Prince had told us about it in great detail. But she said she had never heard of such a thing. I am heartsick. Was Reverend Prince a charlatan? A fake?

I was feeling really blue because I thought Reverend Prince had lied to us about Africa. But Erma wouldn't hear of it. She went straight to Reverend Prince and told him what Miss Franklin had said. She was angry with me for not believing in him.

"After all he's done for us! How could you doubt him?"

Wednesday, October 1, 1919

This very afternoon when school was out, Reverend Prince came to Miss Franklin's room and spoke to her out in the hallway. There was absolutely no way for us to eavesdrop. I don't know how he managed it, but Reverend Prince is going to speak to our class tomorrow.

Thursday, October 2, 1919

Reverend Prince told the entire class about the great kingdoms of Africa: Ghana, Mali, and Songhay of West Africa. He showed us books that had been written long ago in another language called Arabic and then translated into French and then English. He could read the books in French! Can you imagine that?

Everybody was so quiet when Reverend Prince was talking. They had never heard such things before. Erma and I were proud that we knew more than our teacher!

But Miss Franklin listened very attentively. I will not doubt Reverend Prince again. He is not a charlatan.

Saturday, October 4, 1919

We got a letter from Aunt Thannie today. She is coming to spend Thanksgiving with us in Chicago. She didn't say anything about Uncle Meese. I trust he is doing well.

The *Crisis* arrived. Dr. DuBois announced that there will be twelve *Brownie* issues instead of the one per year. Erma and I begged Daddy to let us subscribe to it. But he said he didn't think he could manage it, with the *Crisis* going up to 15 cents in November.

Monday, October 6, 1919

It rained all day. Rosie came up to play with us, because her Mama was busy fixing hair. Miz Hamilton has four regular customers besides Mama, Erma, and me. Mama drew outlines of our hands on paper and then we decorated them with colors. I put a big green ring on my finger. "This is a ruby ring!"

Mama laughed. "Rubies are red," Mama said, "not green."

"Oh! When I grow up and get married and have a daughter, I'm going to name her Ruby," I said.

"I hope she won't be green," Erma said.

Friday, October 10, 1919

Daddy's meeting with Mr. DePriest was this afternoon. We checked Daddy from head to toe to make sure he didn't have a wrinkle anywhere. He drove the short distance to Mr. DePriest's house at 4536 South State Street.

Later

Daddy was home when we got in from school. His face was lit up like a hundred flaming candles. Mr. DePriest said Daddy's paperwork was all in order and he didn't think there would be any problem getting his license.

"Did you have to pay him money?" Mama asked.

"I voluntarily made a donation to his campaign fund. He never asked me for a dime! In fact, he had already promised to help me before I offered to make a donation. It was all very businesslike."

Daddy was so excited he sat down right then and wrote a letter to Papa Till. Each one of us added a line.

Miz Hamilton and Rosie came up to celebrate. So did Mother Doris. "I'm proud of you, Brother Freeman," said Mother Doris. "But I'm hoping that I won't be your first customer. When the time comes, though, I'll let you put these ol' bones in the ground, next to Lester." That was her late husband.

Monday, October 13, 1919

Even though Erma and I are in the same class, we have made separate friends. I like Daisy and Clarice. She likes Juanita and Joyce. All of them are from the South just like us. Daisy and Clarice are both from Arkansas. But I just noticed something. Daisy and Clarice are light-skinned like me. Juanita and Joyce are dark like Erma. I didn't choose them to be my friends for that reason, but I wonder, is that why they chose me? When I told Erma Jean what I thought, she said I was too color conscious. I am not!

Tuesday, October 14, 1919

I didn't go to school today. I don't feel good at all.

Tuesday, October 28, 1919

I've been sick for two weeks — down with the measles. They say I had a terrible fever. Mama blessed the day we came to Chicago because without the care I got at Provident Hospital, I would have been in the ground. I remember very little of the first week — Mama sitting beside my bed, Daddy rubbing my forehead.

Although I am out of danger, I am still weak. All this week, I've been getting better and better. I miss Erma. She's been with Mother Doris, so she wouldn't get infested — no, that should be *infected*. No matter, I was infested with measles all over my body and they itched!

Later

All the people in the building brought me a cake today. Even Mr. and Mrs. Cooper, the new family that moved into the Williams's apartment. Each family donated ingredients, and Mother Doris baked it.

"It's not my birthday," I said.

"We're celebrating 'cause you're going to live," said Rosie. Her mother made her shush! I must have been pretty sick, with people fussing over me so much.

I got the first slice of cake and everybody got a piece. Mother Doris is as good a cook as Grandma Nessie, though I would never tell Grandma Nessie that to her face. I must write and tell Grandma Nessie and Papa Till about the measles and that I am well.

Wednesday, October 29, 1919

I know my sister's footsteps. Mama said it was safe for her to come home. Mama had to make us go to sleep. We couldn't stop talking.

Thursday, October 30, 1919

Reverend Prince came by the house and brought me an orange. I haven't had an orange slice since I've been in Chicago. I don't want to eat it just yet. I love the smell of it.

Friday, October 31, 1919

Daddy still hasn't heard about the license for his funeral home. He is being patient because Mr. DePriest asked him to be.

Although Daddy still works every day, he hates it. He goes to his NAACP meetings at Unity Hall or to the Wabash Avenue YMCA and that keeps him from bursting. Mama stays busy with her suffrage and anti-lynching meetings, too. "I seem to have more time here," she said. "It doesn't take all day to clean three rooms." And of course, our favorite time together is when the *Crisis* comes, and Daddy reads it to us. Last time, he let Erma and me read — just like Papa Till.

Monday, November 3, 1919

I went back to school this morning.

When I got home, Mama made me write thank-you notes to all the neighbors and to my classmates.

I decorated plain paper and made it look very fancy. Then when I made my letters I added squiggles and curls to them. Writing thank-you notes was much more fun than I would have thought. Later Erma helped me put them under each neighbor's door.

Later

We all read the *Crisis* this evening. Even though the cost went up to 15 cents, we still think it is worth it. It has more pages and more pictures.

Tuesday, November 4, 1919

Hooray! Daddy got his license today! He really got it! He was half laughing and half crying when he showed us the papers. Most of all, he was relieved. Daddy sat right down and wrote Papa Till and Grandma Nessie, telling them that Love and Sons Funeral Home, North, was real. Then he took us out to dinner — to a very fashionable restaurant in the heart of the South Side. Mama fussed that she could have prepared the same meal for far less money. "Yes," said Daddy, "but it wouldn't have been so much fun."

Mama couldn't disagree. And neither did Erma or me.

Later

Daddy told us how he is going to quit his job. He's going to put on a suit of clothes, a white shirt and tie, and shine his shoes. Then he's going right into his boss's office and tell him he is leaving to start his own business. To top it off, Daddy is going to give his boss a business card. Oh, I can see it now!

Daddy set the day after Thanksgiving as his opening. It's going to mean a lot of hard work, but he wants to do it, and now I believe that whatever my father wants to do, he will find a way. I'm so proud of him.

"I would love to be a fly on the wall just to see Daddy turn on his heels and strut away from his job," Erma told me later. "Thanks to Mr. DePriest."

One day I hope to thank Mr. DePriest in person.

Saturday, November 8, 1919

Guess who was at the Saturday lecture at the Open Mind Church and Youth Center — Miss Franklin. Yes, she was!

There she was sitting right up front, hanging on every word Reverend Prince was saying.

"You know, the Reverend sure does have the right name," Erma said. "He is a prince!"

"Shame on you," I said, "for thinking like that."

Erma allowed that she wasn't the only one. "Look at how Miss Franklin is looking at him."

Or better still. Look at how he was looking at her. Miss Franklin and Reverend Prince? Goodness.

Monday, November 10, 1919

Daddy took the last of the savings and put it down on a small building over on 35th Street. It needs to be painted and cleaned up, but Daddy thinks it will work out just fine.

Tuesday, November 11, 1919

Today we celebrated the first anniversary of the end of the Big War. I remember how happy we were last year knowing that Uncle Pace and William were going to be coming home soon.

A parade passed right under our window. It brought back memories of Uncle Pace. He should be somewhere marching in a parade as a proud veteran, I thought. But instead he is dead. I didn't feel much like seeing a parade. I would have rather been in school.

Wednesday, November 12, 1919

Miss Franklin announced today that her class has been asked to put on the Thanksgiving program. We are not going to do the traditional program with the pilgrims and the Indians. She has given twenty-six of us a letter in the alphabet. Each letter stands for a person, place, or thing that is from the history of Colored people. I have D for Frederick Douglass. Erma has T for Sojourner Truth. After we tell about our person we all say together: "We are thankful. Are you?" And point to the audience. They are supposed to say, "Yes."

Reverend Prince has been helping out by bringing books from his personal library. Miss Franklin can't seem to stop smiling when Reverend Prince is around.

Wednesday, November 19, 1919

It's a three-nineteen day. November is the eleventh month, so that becomes 11-19-1919. That adds up to five ones and three nines. $5 + 3 = 8$. There are eight more days until our school program.

Friday, November 21, 1919

Between helping Daddy get everything fixed up at his building and working on the school play I haven't had too much time to write. It is so cold — colder than I have ever felt in my life. The wind blowing off the lake takes your breath away.

Aunt Thannie is coming. Says she has heard from Uncle Meese. He's fine, and she will tell us more face-to-face rather than in a letter. Oh goody, she'll be here for the school program.

Saturday, November 22, 1919

Mama always seems to know things. We never said anything, so how did she know we wanted store-bought dresses instead of homemade? She took us to the downtown Sears to buy new coats. They kept a Sears catalog at the general store in the Corners, and sometimes people ordered things from it. But think of it — we were in the real Sears and Roebuck!

Mama bought two coats just alike. Mine is brown tweed and Erma's is green tweed — with muffs to match. I had my eye on a bright red one, but Mama would not even consider it. "Red is just too loud," she said. It's amazing what people think of ordinary colors — red, black, brown, yellow. When I am all grown-up, I will buy myself a red coat and wear it to church! If it was Reverend Prince's church, he wouldn't care.

Mama saw a dress that she liked. It was on sale because it was missing a button. Mama held it up to size it. "Don't you want to try it on?" the saleslady asked.

We were shocked. Was it possible to try on the dress

before buying it? That wouldn't happen in a Southern store — especially in the Corners.

"If you buy a sale garment," the saleslady said, "you can't bring it back."

"Why would Mama buy a dress and then bring it back?" I asked Erma.

Mama shushed me.

Monday, November 24, 1919

Aunt Thannie is here, just in time for the school play. She was talking on and on about an organization she has joined called the Universal Negro Improvement Association headed by a man named Marcus Garvey. "Garvey came here from Jamaica," said Aunt Thannie. "He's only been in Harlem a couple of years, but he's got a large following. I'm proud to be counted among the number who think he's our next great leader!"

"Better than Dr. DuBois and Mrs. Wells-Barnett?" Mama asked.

"You can count on it," said Aunt Thannie.

That is the first we've heard of Marcus Garvey, but Aunt Thannie assures us that we will hear more.

Wednesday, November 26, 1919

Today was the Thanksgiving play. All the parents and teachers and people from the community came. I was so nervous because I didn't want to mess up!

We all did our parts well. Nobody forgot or messed up, not even Booker Jones, the slowest boy in class. But people didn't understand that they were supposed to say YES when we asked, "Are you?" Then it was my turn.

> D is for Frederick Douglass.
> He was a former slave who taught himself to
>   read and write.
> He ran away to freedom and became an abo-
>   litionist.
> He spend his whole life trying to make things
>   fair and equal for all Americans, and that
>   includes me.
> I'm thankful for Frederick Douglass.
> Are you?

When I finished, Aunt Thannie leaped to her feet. "Yes! Yes, I'm thankful for him, honey. You bet I am. And the rest of you ought to be, too." And she sat down. Thank goodness for Aunt Thannie.

By the time we got to H for Hannibal people had caught on. And when we said, "We're thankful. Are you?" The audience all responded with a loud, "Yes!"

When it was over, everybody cheered and clapped their hands. We third graders really know how to put on a good program. Well, thanks to Miss Franklin and Reverend Prince.

Thanksgiving, November 27, 1919

All the people in the building decided that they wanted to have dinner together but it would be impossible to get all of us into one tiny two-room apartment. Then Miz Hamilton had a good idea. She suggested we move all the furniture out of one apartment and set up two rows of tables. "We can all bring a dish."

Daddy quickly volunteered our apartment. Mama made buttermilk pies and candied sweet potatoes. Everybody pitched in and bought a big turkey and Mother Doris roasted it with dressing. The new families brought collards. Doc Kebbs and Virginia brought homemade rolls. It was a feast. But Doc Kebbs had to go on duty, so he took his dessert with him.

Since it was our house, Daddy was chosen to say the prayer. It was short and sincere — much like Daddy.

"We thank thee, Lord, for allowing us to come through so many trials and tribulations and yet not be discouraged. Bless this food and the hands that prepared it. Amen."

After we cleaned up, Aunt Thannie filled us in on what Uncle Meese is doing. He's in Paris getting ready to open another "establishment." Mama likes that word better than *nightclub*. Can you imagine, a Colored club in Paris, France? Seems the French enjoy Colored people's music, dance, art, and books. They welcome Colored artists to come there. It makes sense that Uncle Meese would open a club there, even though Mama gets breathless when she speaks of it.

Friday, November 28, 1919

Daddy opened his funeral home today. He looked mighty distinguished greeting guests at the door. When the people didn't seem to be coming in fast enough, Aunt Thannie stood out front and pulled in folks off the street. "Come on in here," she said. "We all got to come this way one day. So you might as well take a look."

People from the YMCA and the NAACP dropped by, too. And Reverend Prince came and guess who was with him? Miss Franklin! Now that was a surprise.

Even Mr. Link showed up. As big and as strong-looking as he is, Mr. Link was not very comfortable in the funeral home. At last there is something Mr. Link is afraid of.

"I came by," he said, "just to pay my respects."

"Come on in, Mr. Link," Daddy said. "You can be my first customer if you'd like." People think a lot of times that since Daddy's an undertaker he has no sense of humor. But he does. When Mr. Link realized what Daddy had said, his face turned green. "I don't think so," he said. And as soon as he could, he excused himself, but not before asking Aunt Thannie if she'd join him for dinner.

Erma and I got a good laugh out of the idea that four people we like also like each other.

By the end of the day, Daddy had his first funeral, a factory worker.

Later

All afternoon Mama and Daddy kept looking at the door. They were looking for William. I prayed that he'd come. And sure enough he made it. Late, but all that was forgiven the minute we laid eyes on him.

And he's got to leave first thing tomorrow morning,

but we've enjoyed him this evening. Mama fussed at him about not writing, but then he flashed her one of his smiles and she melted.

He brought Erma and me hair ribbons. Oh, William is such a scamp, but I love him so much.

After he polished off two dishes of Mama's peach cobbler, William started telling us stories. Aunt Thannie and Mr. Link were back by that time. We all laughed until tears rolled down our cheeks when he told us about a passenger who worked him to death from Chicago to Los Angeles, then tipped him one thin dime! The life of a Pullman porter is hard work, but William is young and to him it seems like fun.

Listening to him talk, I have come to realize that my brother is likely to always be a rolling stone.

Sunday, November 30, 1919

There were five Sundays in November and a blue moon. When there is a full moon twice in a month, the second one is usually called a blue moon. It doesn't happen often, so that's how come people say things like, "This only happens once in a blue moon," or "It will be a blue moon when that happens."

I am looking up at that full moon as it hangs there in the sky like a big balloon. I wonder what's up there. I wonder what would happen to Moon People if they came down here to visit us. When I asked Erma she just clicked her teeth — just like Mama — and shook her head. "How do you come up with such ideas?"

Monday, December 1, 1919

The Colored Christmas Parade is put on by the Wabash Businessmen's Alliance. Daddy's a part of that group now. It is held every year on the second Sunday in December. The Winter Wonderland Queen is selected by the businessmen. Then each organization selects an attendant called a "snowball maid."

The students in class voted for me to be in the parade to represent the third grade at Dunbar School. All the girls who were selected were light-skinned. So I spoke up. "I don't want to be in the parade. But my sister would like to be!" So I nominated her.

The class voted again and this time they chose Daisy, another light-skinned girl. I couldn't believe even the dark-skinned girls Juanita and Joyce voted for Daisy and not for Erma.

Later

Erma hasn't spoken to me all evening. When I come into the room, she goes out. She cuts me short. What is going on? What did I do?

"Whatever is going on between you two," said Mama, "you had best settle it. We've got trouble all around us. We can't stand if we fight each other."

Tuesday, December 2, 1919

There was a note on my pillow this morning when I woke up. Erma was up and dressed and out already. It said:

> *Sister Dear:*
> *I wish you would stop trying to protect me. You are not Mama. You are my sister. Be a good sister and let me solve my own problems. I didn't need you to nominate me. You didn't even ask. You did what was right for you, without thinking about me. I don't need to be a snowball maid to prove that I'm as pretty as a light-skinned girl. I am writing this because if I tried to tell you, I would lose my nerve.*

Your sister,
Erma Jean

P.S. I am going to use my full name from now on. So call me Erma Jean.

When I went to the door, *Erma Jean* was sitting on the top step. I sat beside her. "I'm so, so sorry," I said. "I just hate prejudiced people — white and Colored."

"I know." And she wiped the tear from my eye, and I wiped the tear from hers. "But it's like Reverend Prince says and Aunt Thannie, too. Being black is not a bad thing. When you try to push me off on people, you make me feel even worse."

"Never again," I promised.

When we looked up, Aunt Thannie was standing in the stairwell. "Are you eavesdropping?" I asked.

"You two are something else," she said. Then, getting her pocketbook, she took us out for a soda.

Thursday, December 4, 1919

Aunt Thannie went home today. We will miss her so much. So will Mother Doris, because Aunt Thannie slept downstairs with her.

Rosie thinks our Aunt Thannie is about as pretty as any lady she has ever seen, especially after she gave Rosie a pretty handkerchief. Aunt Thannie is like that — giving, caring.

Saturday, December 6, 1919

It snowed over ten inches.

Reverend Prince and Miss Franklin are officially courting. But it is all being done quite properly. He visits her at her rooming house where other teachers live. And on Saturdays and Sundays she comes to the Open Mind Church and Youth Center and has begun teaching adults how to read and write.

Today Reverend Prince read us a poem by a new poet named Claude McKay: "If We Must Die." "He wrote this poem because there have been so many lynchings, so much rioting this year all over the country. After the riots here in Chicago," he said, "James Weldon Johnson called 1919 the Red Summer because so much blood has been spilled. But yet we survived — battered and torn, but still standing."

>─┼◆>─O─<◆┼─<

Sunday, December 7, 1919

After church we wrote Christmas letters to all the family. We wrote Papa Till and Grandma Nessie separate letters, so they could each feel like they got something. When I had finished my letter I made a lot of X's and O's. That means love. I wrote to Uncle John Willis and told him I hoped to see him in the summer. Then we could do Miss Mary Mack.

Daddy is very busy trying to keep the business going. He tries to treat people the way he wants to be treated — never forgetting where he came from. Daddy will never get so citified that he'll look down his nose at anybody.

Wednesday, December 10, 1919

You'll never believe who we heard from today. Uncle Meese! It costs 11 cents to send a penny postcard from Paris, France. He'll be home in January.

"I know he'll be happy to get home to his club," said Erma.

Mama gasped. "What do you know about such things?"

"Mama," Erma sighed. "We live in Chicago. What can

we see worse than what we already have seen? Uncle Meese makes an honest living same as Daddy. What's wrong with that?"

Mama stood stone still. I didn't know what she was going to say or do to Erma, being so outspoken. I am usually the one talking out of turn.

At last Mama said, "Well, daughter, that may be true, but I'll keep you a child as long as I can, because childhood is so short. You're going to be grown an awful long time! And not another word about that!"

Saturday, December 13, 1919

Reverend Prince announced that his Saturday and Sunday programs have grown so that he is moving to a new location. When he gave the address, I thought I recognized the number. Then it came to me, the Open Mind Church and Youth Center was going to be located next to Daddy's funeral home.

"If it hadn't been for your father speaking for me, I wouldn't have been able to get the bank loan from Mr. Hill," said Reverend Prince. "How can I ever repay you, Freeman?"

"Pass it on," said Daddy. "Pass it on."

Friday, December 19, 1919

It's the three nineteens again. This is the last time this year I will see those numbers in a date. The next time it happens will be January 20, 2020. I wonder will that year have a blue moon? Wonder what it will be like then. Will there be a Chicago? Will there be a South Side? Will there be prejudice? I hope not.

Today begins the Christmas break from school.

Saturday, December 20, 1919

We had a Christmas play at the new Open Mind Church and Youth Center. I was the angel who appeared to Mary and Elizabeth and Joseph. Erma was selected by the children to play the part of the Virgin Mary. And she didn't need any help from me to get the part. She earned the part because she was good. And nobody stopped her from getting the part because she is dark-skinned. If all the world was like the Open Mind maybe things would be better. Maybe.

William is home, so he got to see us in the play. He won't be here for Christmas but not because he has to work. He is going down home to see Grandma Nessie and Papa Till. "I need to see it through," he said. "I need to go say good-bye to Pace, hug Grandma Nessie's neck, and go fishing with Papa Till."

Sunday, December 21, 1919

We woke this morning to a winter wonderland. Snow had fallen, but the sun was bright. We finally got to wear the big scarves Aunt Thannie brought us. We've also gotten a box from Tennessee. It says DON'T OPEN UNTIL CHRISTMAS. Miz Hamilton and Rosie left to go see family over in Gary, Indiana. They'll be home the day after Christmas.

Monday, December 22, 1919

Doc Kebbs and Virginia left for Nashville. They won't be home until the first of the year. So we wished them a Happy New Year early. Everybody wants to be home with family on that day. I wish we could be home with ours.

Tuesday, December 23, 1919

Mother Doris said that she and her husband spent every Christmas at the YMCA, helping to serve dinner to the homeless and new arrivals from the South. She invited us to join her. Mama and Daddy agreed.

"On Christmas?" I asked.

"Especially because it is Christmas," said Daddy.

Wednesday, December 24, 1919

I'm so homesick I can hardly stand it! Christmas Eve is not right. We aren't in the house that Jasper Love built. We aren't hanging our stockings by the fireplace. We aren't smelling Grandma Nessie's sweet potato pie. We aren't singing and visiting friends. Wonder what Josie James is doing? I will write her when I finish.

Later

Alice Mary and her father, Mr. Bud Simmons, came by the apartment this evening. He had on a clean shirt and pants, and Alice Mary really looked nice. Mr. Simmons gave Daddy a bag of meat, saying, "I just wanted you to know that I think the world of your family — always have," he said. "We got here to Chicago with nothing but what we had on our backs. They burned us out. But by the grace, I got a job and I'm making good at the packinghouse. My children is in school and we got something to eat and enough to share. So I brung you this meat to fill out your Christmas dinner."

Thank you in such cases just doesn't seem like enough. We begged him to let Alice Mary stay a while longer and we ran to get Rosie. We played rock school on the steps and had the best time! And I'm not homesick anymore.

Thursday, December 25, 1919

When Erma Jean and I woke up there was a Christmas tree right in front of the window by our bed.

How had they gotten the tree in the house and decorated without waking us up? It must have been magic, I decided. I hung the little cedar angel Uncle John Willis made me on the Christmas tree. When the holidays are over, I will put it back in my chest.

Our stockings were filled with pecans, an orange, an apple, and a book. On the tree was an envelope addressed to us. Inside was a year's subscription to the *Brownie* magazine, a children's version of the *Crisis*. What a wonderful surprise. Then we opened Grandma Nessie and Papa Till's box. Erma and I got lovely lace collars Grandma Nessie had made to cover our dresses. Mama got a lace-trimmed handkerchief. And Daddy got a pipe, hand-carved by Uncle John Willis. There was a picture of Uncle Boston, Celia, and all the children gathered around them. Mama held the picture and just looked at it for the longest time. "I bet they're keeping everybody busy," she said.

In the very bottom of the box was an envelope to us from Papa Till. Inside was a shiny dime.

I know it is hard for them not having us there. Their letter sounded cheerful, but in between the written words were the invisible words: "We miss you, we miss you, we miss you, we miss you."

Later

As was planned, we worked at the YMCA. I helped to set the table, and Erma Jean sliced cake and put it on plates. I couldn't help but think that a few months ago we were new to Chicago, not knowing anybody. We were so impressed with how much Rosie knew. Now we were telling wide-eyed children from Alabama and Mississippi about the wonders of Chicago.

Sunday, December 28, 1919

Today Erma Jean and I are the same age again.

There's only one thing wrong with being born in December. Your birthday gets overlooked. Nobody has said a thing all day about it being my birthday.

Later

What a surprise! Mama sent me down to Mother Doris's apartment. When I walked in all of my friends were there — Rosie, Daisy, Clarice, Alice Mary, and others from the Open Mind Church and Youth Center. They all shouted Happy Birthday! I have never had a surprise birthday party. I got a pencil and a pad, a horn, a handkerchief, a whistle, and a lovely store-bought card from Mother Doris. It was wonderful!

Wednesday, December 31, 1919

It's hard to believe the year is over and it is time to start a new diary. This one will always be special to me, because it is my first. Just think, I didn't even want to write in a diary. But every page is filled. So much has happened in a year's time.

I will never forget 1919 — the year of the Red Summer — as long as I live. But as terrible as it was — the death of Uncle Pace, the loss of Erma's voice, the move to Chicago, the riots, the prejudices — I have happy memories, too. Daddy's business is picking up. He just put a down payment on a motor hearse. It will be delivered in February. Mama is still working hard in the suffrage movement — handing out pamphlets and attending meetings. She is not as timid or shy as she used to be, but she is always a lady, very proper even during the worst of times.

Whenever I hear Reverend Prince speak to a room full of people, I think of how he started with just a handful of us. Daddy finally broke down and joined the church. So we go to Open Mind on Saturday and Sunday. I wouldn't be surprised if Miss Franklin becomes Mrs. Prince McDonald very soon, too. She wouldn't be our teacher anymore, but she could still be our friend. I'd settle for that.

Later

Chicago is big and dirty and it smells bad. But here Colored people have a chance. They come here because they and their children are able to hope for something a little better. Oh, I miss the green grass under my feet. I miss the sound of birds chattering and squirrels squabbling in our big tree out back in the Corners. But there is never a dull moment outside our living room window here in Chicago. I can sit out front and see more life in an hour than most people in the Corners experience all year. I miss the river and swimming in the lake, but I've got the lake here instead. Chicago is very different from Bradford Corners. If I had to live in either place alone, I would be sad. But wherever my father and mother and Erma Jean are, it's all right. We are family and that's how we make it, and we'll keep on making it as long as we pull together and love each other no matter what!

Epilogue

Freeman Love became a prominent undertaker in Chicago. He moved his family into one of the finest homes on East 42nd Street within three years' time. Although Freeman ran for public office several times, he was never elected. However, he brought attention to the high level of corruption among public officials, which caused several investigations.

Olive Love was proud to be the first woman in her family to cast a ballot when the U.S. Constitution was amended in 1920, allowing women to vote. During prohibition in the 1920s, Uncle Meese lost his club, but he moved to Paris where he opened several cabarets.

Grandma Nessie and Papa Till died within months of each other in 1926. They never ventured out of the Corners, although they welcomed all relatives. The house that Jasper Love built is still standing. There is a larger, more modern mortuary next door where the carriage house used to be. Boston Love, with the help of John Willis Love, ran it until he retired and two of his sons are still managing it today. The motto is still "Faith, Hope, and Love."

Aunt Thannie became a Garveyite and strongly supported the Back-to-Africa Movement. Reverend Prince McDonald married Miss Franklin and continued to build the Open Mind Church and Youth Center, serving the masses of poor people who poured into Chicago between 1919 and 1945.

Erma Jean Love grew up to become a well-known, award-winning poet and playwright. After working four summers in the *Crisis* office in New York, she graduated from New York University with a major in English and French. One of her books, based on her experiences during the Red Summer, became a hit play in the 1960s. Erma Jean spent most of her time in Paris where she took care of business for her aging Uncle Meese. She married Vincent Trudeau, a French artist, and they had two daughters, Jeannie and Leigh. But she always maintained an apartment in Chicago.

William Love settled down, married, and lived the remainder of his life in California where he became a teacher.

Nellie Lee Love graduated from Howard University in Washington, D.C., and married Robert Jennings, a judge. She was employed in the White House during the

Roosevelt administration. She worked very closely with Mrs. Eleanor Roosevelt, who often asked Nellie Lee's advice on issues of race and race relations. It was Nellie Lee who brought it to her attention that all of the Colored women who worked in the secretarial pool were fair-skinned. Within a few weeks, a woman was hired who was darker. And in the 1960s when others around her resisted using the term "black," Nellie Lee embraced it. "I am a black woman," she said during a television interview.

When Nellie Lee Love Jennings died in 1991, her granddaughter spoke at her funeral, saying she was a fighter. She fought for justice, peace, and equality. "Grandma Nellie Lee taught me that family is important. I can hear her saying, 'With a family behind you, standing with you, surrounding you with love, then you become an immovable force.' I believed my grandmother, as I hope my granddaughter will believe me when I tell her the same thing." Nellie Lee was a proud black woman who was quick to tell you that she was the great-granddaughter of Jasper Love, whose house was built on a solid foundation of faith, hope, and unconditional love. It still stands.

In a small cemetery in Bradford Corners, Tennessee, where she is buried near her beloved ancestors, Nellie Lee's gravestone is clearly marked: *Color Me Dark!*

Life in America
in 1919

Historical Note

>–I–‹›–◯–‹›–I–‹

Between World War I and World War II, over 3.5 million African Americans migrated from the rural South to the great urban centers in the Midwest, North, and Northeast. The first of three migratory waves called the "Great Migration" began in 1919. Why did black people leave the South in record numbers during that particular year? The reasons varied from person to person, and family to family. But the common motivator seems to have been hope. The industrial North offered young men the hope of better jobs. Countless mothers left their childhood homes behind, hoping that in the North they would find better health care and schooling for their children. Professional, well-educated people closed up shops and traveled north filled with hopes and dreams of unlimited opportunity. For millions of poor sharecroppers, the North was the Promised Land — a place where they could dare hope to live in safety and freedom from the day-to-day grind of poverty, humiliation, and degradation.

Until 1919, the movement of blacks out of the South

was steady, but there hadn't been a dramatic shift in the population since the decades after the Civil War. After World War I, things changed drastically.

The war ended November 11, 1918. Approximately 370,000 black soldiers and officers had served in the military and over half of this number fought valiantly in well-known battles. Back in the United States, however, racist groups, such as the Ku Klux Klan, had begun to spread fear that black soldiers had forgotten their place. And the only way to keep them under control, the Klan preached, was to use fear, force, and violence.

In 1918, sixty-three people were lynched. In 1919, many of them were black soldiers recently home from the army. In addition, there were twenty-five race riots in Northern and Southern cities. One of the longest riots was in Chicago.

The Chicago Riot began July 27, 1919, at a beach along Lake Michigan. A black teenager drowned as a result of being attacked. White bathers threw rocks at him when he accidentally floated into an all-white swimming area. When the police refused to arrest those whites who had stoned the boy, a large number of blacks gathered to protest. There was shoving, pushing, and a shot was fired. What followed was two weeks of off-and-on rioting. In most cities, blacks hid in their homes while angry white mobs burned the homes and businesses. In Chicago, however, something was different. African Americans defended the homes and shops and stores from lawless gangs. They fought back. James Weldon Johnson, the executive director of the National Association for the Advancement of Colored People (the NAACP) called it the "Red Summer" because so much blood was spilled.

The riots in Northern cities didn't stop the flow of northern migration. The rise of Klan violence, poor jobs, and limited opportunities was enough to offset the riots, and blacks poured into Philadelphia, Newark, New York, Boston, Cleveland, Indianapolis, St. Louis, Detroit, and Chicago in unprecedented numbers.

The National Association for the Advancement of Colored People, started in 1909 by a group of whites and blacks, is one of the oldest civil rights organizations still operating today. Its original purpose was to use every available legal avenue to achieve equality under the law for all Americans. In 1919, the focus of the NAACP was on getting an anti-lynching law passed in Congress.

James Weldon Johnson (1871–1938) was a lawyer, statesman, educator, and poet. His poem, written in 1900, "Lift Ev'ry Voice and Sing," was set to music by his brother, Rosamond Johnson. The song was designated by the NAACP as "The Negro National Anthem."

Although Johnson held a powerful position within the NAACP, Dr. W.E.B. DuBois's voice was one of the most influential in the nation. DuBois (1868–1963) was born in Great Barrington, Massachusetts, to a long line of free blacks. He was educated at Fisk University in Nashville, Tennessee, and at Harvard University where he earned a Ph.D. He devoted his life to the abolition of racial inequality within the American system of government.

DuBois became the editor of the *Crisis,* the publishing arm of the NAACP, and it was through this publication — and other black media — that black people were informed about events that were rarely, if ever, featured in the white media. Southern whites imposed an unwritten ban on the NAACP and the *Crisis.* Any person suspected of belonging to the NAACP — white or black — ran the risk of being fired from his or her job or of being intimidated by the Klan. Yet blacks and a few southern whites secretly paid their dues and subscribed to the *Crisis.*

DuBois continued his work as an activist until he died in 1963 on the eve of the March on Washington where Martin Luther King, Jr., made his famous "I Have a Dream" speech.

Another founder of the NAACP and a prominent national leader was Ida B. Wells-Barnett (1862–1931). Born in Mississippi, after attending Rust College, Ida B.Wells moved to Memphis, Tennessee, and took a job with a newspaper, the *Memphis Free Speech*. In 1882, at the age of twenty, Wells became a part owner of that paper. She made many enemies when, in her outspoken editorials, she challenged segregation as unconstitutional. She sued and won a case against a conductor for physically throwing her off a streetcar when she refused to sit in an all-black section. She protested against inferior black schools and public facilities.

Then, in May 1892, the *Free Speech* newspaper office was burned and Wells barely escaped being attacked. Friends encouraged her to go north where it would be safer for her to carry on her work. Her situation was quite dangerous, for in 1892, forty-nine blacks were reported lynched, and a number of those victims were women.

Ida B.Wells went to New York and then Chicago. She began her campaign against lynching and violence, and through careful research she was able to document the horrific loss of lives. She married Ferdinand Barnett, an editor, lawyer, and businessman, who encouraged her to work for women's suffrage. She organized the Ida B.

Wells Women's Club of Chicago in 1895, and the Alpha Suffrage Club in 1913. Through these two organizations black women all over the country organized and presented a united front in a common cause.

Chicago was founded by a black man by the name of Jean Baptiste Pointe du Sable (1745–1818). Born in Haiti to a black woman and a French mariner, Du Sable was educated in France. He came to New Orleans as a free man and followed the waterways north to a portage between the Chicago and Des Plaines rivers. There he set up a trading post from which the city of Chicago developed .

The story of Madam C. J. Walker (1867–1919) was well-known throughout the black community — North and South. Sarah Breedlove had been born poor and grew up motherless in Mississippi. Moving to St. Louis when she was sixteen, Sarah became a washerwoman. In 1903, she developed a hair care product and a system that helped black women manage their hair. Locating her office in Indianapolis, Sarah married C. J. Walker and changed her name to Madam C. J. Walker. Before her death in 1919, Madam Walker had helped over 2,000 agents earn an independent living by selling her products. And, in the process, she had amassed a fortune. Madam C. J. Walker had become America's first self-made black millionaire.

Dr. Daniel Hale Williams (1856–1931) was the founder of Provident Hospital, located on the South Side of Chicago. Many rural Southern blacks died because they lacked basic health care. Dr. Williams was determined to establish a hospital where medical professionals could be trained to set up facilities in black communities all over the country.

Dr. Williams was born in Hollidayburg, Pennsylvania, in 1856. He was educated at Chicago Medical College and completed his degree in 1883. After managing a successful private practice, Dr. Williams saw the need for a good black hospital. He raised the money to start Provident Hospital and Training School Association, which opened its doors in January 1891. Provident was the first hospital founded and fully controlled by African Americans.

A landmark medical event took place at Provident on July 9, 1893. Dr. Williams performed open-heart surgery on a man who had been shot. He opened the man's chest cavity and surgically repaired the puncture in the pericardium (the sac) surrounding the heart. It was a medical triumph.

Oscar DePriest (1871–1951) was born in Florence, Alabama, but his family moved to Kansas when he was young. DePriest made his way to Chicago as a young man and earned a small fortune in the real estate business. In 1928, DePriest was the first African American since Reconstruction to be elected to the United States House of Representatives.

Robert Abbott's (1870–1940) success story is equally as impressive as the ones before him. Born on St. Simon Island off the coast of Georgia, Abbott studied at Beach Institute in Savannah and later attended Claflin College in South Carolina. After migrating to Chicago, he published his first edition of the *Chicago Defender* on May 5, 1905. He sold it door-to-door, and soon it became one of the most widely-read black newspapers in the country, along with the *Amsterdam News* of Harlem and the *Pittsburgh Courier*.

It was through advertisements in the *Defender* that many Southern blacks learned about job opportunities in Chicago slaughterhouses, stockyards, and railroads. They flocked to the city in large numbers.

Blacks weren't the only ones to be drawn to the North in search of a better life. Poor Southern whites came north looking for the same opportunities for themselves.

Some well-established white families wanted nothing to do with poor whites. And, ironically, some upper-class blacks had the same attitude toward poor blacks. Arriving in Chicago for the first time, blacks were pleased to know that they could shop and ride the streetcars and move about the city with relative ease. There was far less overt racism than in the South. But there was plenty of class bias.

The social stratification in Chicago was rigid and unmovable, especially within the black community, where newcomers were viewed as "spoilers" who brought disgrace on the race with their lack of culture and sophistication. The "Black Elite," usually mulattos who were wealthy and well-educated, distanced themselves from the masses by retreating into restricted private social clubs and organizations where members were handpicked.

Unfortunately, many poor whites brought their racist attitudes north with them. Feeling rejected and alienated, some Southern youths formed groups known as "athletic clubs," and they roamed the streets harassing blacks and immigrants. This gave them the illusion that they were better than others. The emergence of the "Black Elite" was only an illusion, too, for in the end, even though they were rich and perhaps well connected, they were still black and in America that meant they were still second-class citizens. Elitism served only to divide the black community and created a class system that caused the poor to mistrust the leadership of some capable blacks who had their best interests at heart.

In time, many Southerners went back "down home." They returned to the South, happy to be back among people who knew their names. Others stayed in Chicago and other Northern industrial centers and became successful. And by 1938, when another wave of blacks came North, those who had migrated in 1919 were now the ones looking down their noses at the new arrivals fresh off the train, wide-eyed and terrified. A large number of those who migrated remained poor, undereducated, and at the bottom of the social, political, and economic ladder. For them the promise was not fulfilled. For them hope had died.

A leader who understood the power of a unified front against the pressures of urban living was Marcus Garvey (1887–1940). He is often called a "racial nationalist." Born in Jamaica, Garvey came to Harlem in 1916 and established the Universal Negro Improvement Association that promoted black self-help, pride, and love. Although he is best remembered for his "Back-to-Africa" position, those who followed him also appreciated his lessons in blackness and pride. Unfortunately, Garvey was deported in 1926. He died in England on June 10, 1940. But he influenced a whole generation of people who were not willing to remain passive and uninvolved. One of Garvey's followers was Delores Little, the mother of Malcolm Little who became Malcolm X, a leader who also spoke to the hearts of urban blacks.

After WWI, conditions in the South worsened. Black soldiers returned home to threats, lynching, and a suffering economy. Many people moved north to escape racism, find better work, and to better educate and care for their children.

Many men transplanted their entire families to the North. Upon arrival in Chicago, some families had already arranged for accommodations and employment. Others had to start from nothing.

Quite different from the rural dirt roads and outhouses of the South, Chicago was a bustling city with wide streets, fancy cars, and indoor plumbing.

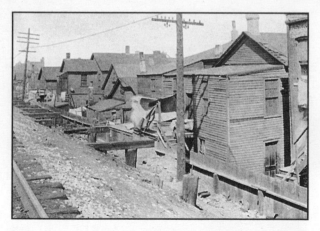

Some families were struck by the cold reality that poverty ran rampant in the North as well. Southern families that once lived in houses with many rooms found themselves in small, one-bedroom, tenement apartments that met only the most basic standards of living.

Chicago's more established black families were able to afford much more luxurious homes. Often, these richer, more cosmopolitan blacks looked down on poor, uneducated emigrants — both black and white.

The CRISIS

THE
AMERICAN NEGRO'S RECORD IN THE GREAT
WORLD WAR

LOYALTY
VALOR
ACHIEVEMENT

ONE DOLLAR A YEAR   MAY 1919   TEN CENTS A COPY

From 1910–1932, W.E.B. DuBois was the editor of the Crisis, *a publication of the National Association for the Advancement of Colored People (NAACP). In it, he sought to inform black people about issues affecting their lives. Many Southerners learned about the opportunities in the North and the struggle for black rights through their subscriptions to the* Crisis *and other northern publications such as the* Chicago Defender, *the* Amsterdam News, *and the* Pittsburgh Courier.

W.E.B. DuBois believed that only through education could blacks gain status in American society. He wrote many books and essays expressing his beliefs about racial assimilation, cooperation, and the use of education to end prejudice. Perhaps his greatest achievement, however, was the formation of the National Association for the Advancement of Colored People (NAACP), which he founded in 1909 along with other black and white leaders. He was later part of the American Delegation to the founding meeting of the United Nations along with Eleanor Roosevelt, Mary McLeod Bethune, and Walter White.

In the summer of 1919, racial tensions mounted in Chicago. One incident triggered an onslaught of violent race riots where white mobs burned and ravaged the homes and businesses of blacks. That summer has been dubbed "Red Summer" because so much blood was shed. While some blacks hid in their homes and businesses, others chose to protect and defend their property. In an attempt to keep peace, the police randomly questioned blacks who were on the streets, often escorting them back to their homes.

Here, blacks leave their home under the protection of police. Because their home had been wrecked by looters during the riots, they needed a safe place to stay.

Ida B. Wells-Barnett was born a slave in Holly Springs, Mississippi. She moved to Memphis, Tennessee, in 1884 where she first began her career as a leader and an activist. Later, she moved to New York and then Chicago to escape the threat of lynching. There, she continued to challenge lynching and the constitutionality of segregation, but found her loudest voice in the fight for women's suffrage.

Lynching was the arbitrary and illegal hanging of a person by a mob. Often, African Americans were the victims of white lynch mobs. The growing dissatisfaction of the black people led them to present a united front against lynching. The determination of the black community to organize and protest on this level marked the beginning of the national Civil Rights Movement that would eventually guarantee black Americans the same rights under the Constitution as all other Americans.

Marcus Garvey was born in Jamaica, but came to America with his Universal Negro Improvement and Conservation Association and African Communities League (UNIA) in 1916. His goal was to improve the status of urban black communities. Often called a "racial nationalist," he encouraged black emigration to Africa. Garvey became a symbol of black freedom as his powerful message gave pride and hope to thousands of working-class blacks around the world.

Mr. John Cooper's
Buttermilk Pie

Melt a stick of butter and mix with 2 cups
of sugar in a medium bowl.
Add 3 whole eggs and
2 heaping tablespoons of flour.
Stir mixture until smooth.
Fold in 1 cup of buttermilk.
Stir again until smooth.
Add a dash of nutmeg and a bit of vanilla.
Pour into an unbaked 9-inch pie shell.

Bake 45 minutes at 350°
or until a toothpick inserted in the middle
comes out clean.
Serves 6 to 8.

Pullman dining car chefs were well-known for their unique and delicious pastries and desserts. Passengers traveling from Chicago to New York would have been familiar with Mr. John Cooper's buttermilk pies.

Lift Ev'ry Voice and Sing

Lift every voice and sing
Till earth and heaven ring,
Ring with the harmonies of Liberty;
Let our rejoicing rise
High as the listening skies,
Let it resound loud as the rolling sea.
Sing a song full of the faith that the dark past has taught us,
Sing a song full of the hope that the present has brought us,
Facing the rising sun of our new day begun
Let us march on till victory is won.

Stony the road we trod,
Bitter the chastening rod,
Felt in the days when hope unborn had died;
Yet with a steady beat,
Have not our weary feet
Come to the place for which our fathers sighed?
We have come over a way that with tears has been watered,
We have come, treading our path through the blood of the slaughtered,
Out from the gloomy past,
Till now we stand at last
Where the white gleam of our bright star is cast.

God of our weary years,
God of our silent tears,
Thou who has brought us thus far on the way;
Thou who has by Thy might
Led us into the light,
Keep us forever in the path, we pray.
Lest our feet stray from the places, Our God, where we met Thee,
Lest, our hearts drunk with the wine of the world, we forget Thee;
Shadowed beneath Thy hand,
May we forever stand.
True to our GOD,
True to our native land.

>——I——‹›——O——‹›——I——<

Written by NAACP leader James Weldon Johnson for a presentation in celebration of the birthday of Abraham Lincoln, "Lift Ev'ry Voice and Sing" was originally a poem. It was later set to music by his brother J. Rosamond Johnson and designated "The Negro National Anthem." It was originally performed in Jacksonville, Florida, by children.

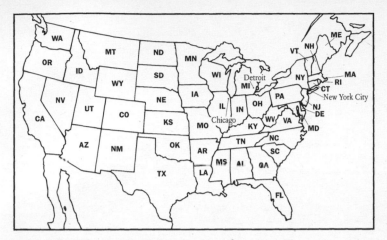

In the early 1900s many black people migrated from the South to major northern cities in search of a better economy, better education, and safety from the lynching in the South. They settled in places like Chicago, Detroit, and New York City.

About the Author

>–!–‹›–⊙–‹›–!–‹

This is Patricia C. McKissack's second book in the Dear America series. Her first title in the series, *A Picture of Freedom: The Diary of Clotee, A Slave Girl*, was a popular title that was successfully made into an HBO Special.

The idea for *Color Me Dark*, which takes place in 1919, grew out of a family story. "One set of grandparents lived in Nashville and the other set lived in St. Louis, so I held dual citizenship in both Missouri and Tennessee," says McKissack. She goes on to explain. "While growing up, I heard my St. Louis grandfather tell stories about how he and his brother had left Nashville at seventeen and eighteen, going to Chicago in search of opportunity. They got there just in time for a terrible riot. It wasn't until many years later that I realized that my grandfather and his brother had been in the city during the Chicago Riot of 1919. When asked how he survived those trying times, my grandfather used one word: 'family.'"

It is out of her commitment to learning and sharing her cultural history and her personal devotion to family that makes this one of McKissack's most sensitive books.

"This is about a dark period in American history. I learned very early that life is not always good or fair or honest or just. But giving up should never be an option."

McKissack has authored over eighty books for young readers. What makes this one different? "I have mirrored some of my own experiences through the eyes of Nellie Lee in a very close-up and personal point of view."

Even though the characters in this are fictional, their story is a real one. McKissack says, "I hope the Love family will show young readers that difficult situations can be overcome by education, kindness, dedication and, above all, love."

Patricia C. McKissack is also the award-winning author of *Flossie and the Fox; Mirandy and Brother Wind*, a Caldecott Honor Book; *The Dark-Thirty: Southern Tales of the Supernatural*, a Newbery Honor Book; and *Christmas in the Big House, Christmas in the Quarters*, a Coretta Scott King Award-winner for text.

Black Hands, White Sails is her most recent Scholastic title, co-authored with her husband, Fredrick McKissack. She has also co-authored a book with her son, Fredrick McKissack Jr., *Black Diamond*. Fred Jr., lives in Chicago. Pat and Fred Sr., live in Chesterfield, Missouri. When she isn't traveling for research, she travels for fun.

Acknowledgments

>-┼-<┼>-┼-O-┼-<┼>-┼-<

Grateful acknowledgment is made for permission to reprint the following:

Cover Portrait: A detail from James Chapin's *Ruby Green Singing*, 1928. Oil on canvas. Norton Museum of Art.

Cover Background: South Water Street in Chicago, Corbis.

Page 201 (top): Waiting to go north. Colored Waiting Room in Union Terminal; Jacksonville, Florida, 1921. Florida State Archives.

Page 201 (bottom): A Negro family, just arrived in Chicago from the south, *The Negro in Chicago: A Study of Race Relations and a Race Riot*, University of Chicago Press, 1922, Schomburg Center for Research in Black Culture, New York Public Library.

Page 202 (top): Policeman directing downtown Chicago traffic, ca. 1917. Corbis.

Page 202 (bottom): Tenements on Federal Street, Chicago, 1920. *The Negro in Chicago: A Study of Race Relations and a Race Riot*, University of Chicago Press, 1922, Schomburg Center for Research in Black Culture, New York Public Library.

Page 203: Wealthy black housing, Schomburg Center for Research in Black Culture, New York Public Library.

Page 204: The *Crisis*, ibid.

Page 205: W.E.B. Dubois, Brown Brothers.

Page 206 (top): Mounted police during race riots, 1919, Corbis/UPI.

Page 206 (bottom): Negroes under protection of police in riot zone, from *The*

Negro in Chicago: A Study of Race Relations and a Race Riot, University of Chicago Press, 1922, Schomburg Center for Research in Black Culture, New York Public Library.

Page 207 (top): Ida B. Wells, Schomburg Center for Research in Black Culture, New York Public Library.

Page 207 (bottom): Anti-lynching protest, Corbis/UPI.

Page 208: Marcus Garvey, ibid.

Page 210: "Lift Ev'ry Voice and Sing," Words by James Weldon Johnson, music by Rosamond Johnson, 1900.

Page 211: Map by Heather Saunders

OTHER BOOKS IN THE DEAR AMERICA SERIES

>─┼─◆─·─O─·─◆─┼─◄

West to a Land of Plenty
The Diary of Teresa Angelino Viscardi
by Jim Murphy

Dreams in the Golden Country
The Diary of Zipporah Feldman
by Kathryn Lasky

A Line in the Sand
The Alamo Diary of Lucinda Lawrence
by Sherry Garland

Standing in the Light
The Captive Diary of Catherine Carey Logan
by Mary Pope Osborne

Voyage on the Great *Titanic*
The Diary of Margaret Ann Brady
by Ellen Emerson White

My Heart Is on the Ground
The Diary of Nannie Little Rose, a Sioux Girl
by Ann Rinaldi

The Great Railroad Race
The Diary of Libby West
by Kristiana Gregory

The Girl Who Chased Away Sorrow
The Diary of Sarah Nita, a Navajo Girl
by Ann Turner

A Light in the Storm
The Civil War Diary of Amelia Martin
by Karen Hesse

A Coal Miner's Bride
The Diary of Anetka Kaminska
by Susan Campbell Bartoletti

WHILE THE EVENTS DESCRIBED AND SOME OF THE CHARACTERS
IN THIS BOOK MAY BE BASED ON ACTUAL HISTORICAL EVENTS
AND REAL PEOPLE, NELLIE LEE LOVE IS A FICTIONAL CHARACTER,
CREATED BY THE AUTHOR, AND HER JOURNAL AND ITS EPILOGUE
ARE WORKS OF FICTION.

>─┤‹›─○─‹›┤─<

Copyright © 2000 by Patricia C. McKissack. All rights reserved. Published by
Scholastic Inc. SCHOLASTIC and associated logos are trademarks
and/or registered trademarks of Scholastic Inc.

ISBN 0-439-52911-5

12 11 10 9 8 7 6 5 4 3 2 1   3 4 5 6 7 8/0

Printed in the U.S. A.   40

First Scholastic Club printing, March 2003

The display type was set in Bernhard Bold Condensed
The text type was set in Fournier MT
Book Design by Elizabeth B. Parisi
Photo research by Zoe Moffitt and Leslie Willis

Originally published in hardcover, April 2000

>─┤‹›─○─‹›┤─<